SAMANTHA BENEKE

The Partner

Book 2 In the Captive Hearts series

Cover design by Samantha Beneke
Stock photography licensed from Pexels and iStock
For more information about the author visit:
www.samanthabenekeromanceauthor.com

First edition

ISBN (print): 978-1-0671074-1-3
ISBN (digital): 978-1-0671074-3-7

This book was professionally typeset on Reedsy.
Find out more at reedsy.com

Contents

THE PARTNER

Book 2 In The Captive Hearts Series
By Samantha Beneke

Author's Note

Reading Order

The Partner is the second book in the Captive Hearts Series and should be read in sequential order for the best reading experience:

- The Pet (Book 1)
- The Partner (Book 2)
- The One (Book 3)

This book picks up directly where *The Pet* ends and contains major spoilers for the first book. New readers should begin with *The Pet* to fully understand the characters' journey and relationship development.

A Note on the Cliffhanger

This book ends on a significant cliffhanger that directly sets up the events 'of Book 3. While the romantic relationship reaches a satisfying emotional resolution, the overarching plot concludes with unresolved tension that will be addressed in The One.

Content Warnings

This book is intended for mature readers (18+) and contains the following potentially triggering content:

- Explicit sexual scenes between consenting adults
- Profanity
- Vampire violence and supernatural abilities
- Psychological manipulation and mind control

- Threats of death and execution
- Blood consumption
- Abduction and kidnapping
- Past trauma and its effects on relationships
- Surveillance and violation of privacy

The Pet: A Recap

Kate Morgan is an emerging artist from New York celebrating her first exhibition in Budapest. Devon Karlov, a centuries-old vampire and art collector, attends her show not just as an admirer of art, but as someone who has secretly obsessed over Kate for the past three years.

That night, Devon took Kate from her hotel room, bringing her to his elegant estate, where she discovered a world she never knew existed—a vampire society with ancient rules, rigid hierarchies, and disturbing traditions. In this world, humans serve vampires as Pets, wearing collars as symbols of their status and submission.

But Kate was never meant to be anyone's Pet.

Turned centuries ago by his maker, Elisabeta, Devon was transformed from mortal to captive immortal. Elisabeta had been both creator and teacher, shaping Devon's early understanding of what it meant to be vampire. But like many maker-child relationships in the vampire world, theirs was complex, marked by power dynamics that would influence Devon's approach to relationships for centuries to come.

Kate refused to wear the collar that vampire law demanded. Her defiance both frustrated and fascinated Devon, who had never encountered anyone who couldn't be owned—not since his own transformation under Elisabeta's guidance.

As their relationship deepened, Devon found himself changing. The vampire who always took what he wanted began asking for permission. He learned the difference between owning and cherishing, but their growing love faced treacherous obstacles. Aleksander, an old vampire acquaintance of Devon's, believes that humans exist to serve as blood banks and covets Kate for his own personal and political gain. The Midwinter Conclave, a gathering of the vampire elite, became a test of wills where Kate walked among ancient vampires as the only human without a collar.

By the end of their story, Kate and Devon have found a rare love built on choice rather than force, respect rather than dominance, and mutual surrender rather than conquest. Yet when Kate stumbles upon an open gate one day, she finds herself needing to make a choice: Walk through the gate and away from Devon, everything they have built, or stay.

Playlist

The Desperate Kingdom Of Love - **PJ Harvey**
Adore You - **Miley Cyrus**
Pug - **Smashing Pumpkins**
Pain For Fun (featuring St. Vincent) - **WILLOW**
Big Jet Plane - **Angus & Julia Stone**
Fresh Blood - **Eels**
Crash Boom Bang - **Roxette**
Do You Remember - **Jarryd James**
Missed - **PJ Harvey**
All I Wanted - **Paramore**
All I Need - **Radiohead**
Adore Me - **Submoons**
Every Other Freckle - **Alt J**
You Are The Ocean - **Phantogram**
The Offering - **Sleep Token**
Army of the Sun - **Roadrunner United**
We're In This Together - **Nine Inch Nails**
I Will Follow You Into The Dark - **Death Cab For Cutie**
Last Goodbye - **Jeff Buckley**
liMOusIne - **Bring Me The Horizon (feat. AURORA)**

Listen to the playlist on Spotify

Dedication

To everyone who has learned that trust isn't given—it's built, one honest moment at a time.

Chapter 1

The dream always began the same way.

Devon stood in the grand ballroom of Elisabeta's Prague estate, the chandeliers casting fractured light across marble floors that reflected like black water. The room was filled with vampires—ancient ones, their faces pale, beautiful and utterly without mercy. But his eyes were drawn, as they always were, to her.

Elisabeta stood at the center of it all, glittering in midnight blue silk that seemed to absorb the light around her. Her dark hair was swept up in an elaborate style that emphasized the elegant line of her neck, and when she smiled, her fangs caught the chandelier's glow like diamonds.

"My dear Devon," she said, her voice carrying easily across the vast space despite its soft tone. "Come to me.

He tried to resist. In the dream, he always tried to resist. But his feet moved against his will, carrying him across the ballroom floor while the other vampires watched with cruel amusement. They knew what was coming; they had seen this performance before.

"You have a choice to make," Elisabeta said when he reached her, her pale hand coming up to trace the line of his jaw with deceptive gentleness. "As you always do."

The ballroom shifted around them, the walls dissolving into the stone corridors of her dungeons. Two malnourished figures knelt in chains before them—a young woman with terrified eyes and a man who looked barely out of his teens. Both human, both innocent.

"Choose," Elisabeta whispered, her breath cool against his ear. "Which one dies quickly, and which one suffers? You must choose, my darling, or I'll make them

both suffer for hours."

"Please," Devon heard himself say, the word torn from his throat. "Don't make me—"

"But I am making you," she replied, her voice like silk over steel. "Because you belong to me, Devon. Your choices belong to me. Your will belongs to me." Her fingers tightened on his jaw, nails digging into his skin. "You will always be mine."

The humans' terrified sobs echoed off the stone walls as Devon's hand rose, trembling, to point at—

Devon Karlov woke with a jolt, his hand instinctively reaching across the bed. The sheets beside him were cold and empty. Kate was gone.

He rose in one fluid motion, not bothering with clothes beyond the silk pajama bottoms he wore. The evening had just begun, the sun having set perhaps an hour ago, casting the room in deep blue shadows that reminded him too much of Elisabeta's gown.

"Kate?" he called, his voice echoing through the high-ceilinged bedroom. No answer.

The silence felt wrong, charged with the same menace that had filled his dream. Devon moved through the suite, checking the bathroom, the adjoining sitting room, the small kitchenette where Kate sometimes made tea in the evenings. Each empty space amplified his growing unease, the nightmare's grip tightening around his chest.

Had Kate left him? The thought tore through him, made worse by the lingering terror of his dream. The bitter irony was not lost on him. After everything they'd been through—her captivity, her escape attempt, their nights in his tomb, the confrontation with Aleksander—had she finally decided that a life with him was too much?

He dressed quickly, pulling on a simple black shirt and trousers, not bothering with shoes. He ran his hands through his black hair to tame it, his blue eyes reflecting anxiety from the mirror in front of him. The marble floors were cool beneath his feet as he strode through the corridors of the estate, calling her name with increasing urgency.

"Kate? Kate, where are you?"

The art studio was empty; her latest canvas half-finished with oils still wet from her work earlier that day. The library showed no signs of her evening reading habit. The kitchen staff hadn't seen her.

Devon's pace quickened as he moved through the grand hall and out onto the terrace. The evening air was crisp, carrying the scent of flowers and distant rain. His eyes scanned the gardens, the pathways, the distant tree line, his vampire vision cutting easily through the gathering darkness.

Then he saw her.

Kate stood at the main gate, her slender figure silhouetted against the wrought iron. She wore one of his white shirts, oversized on her frame, paired with simple black leggings. Her dark brown hair was loose around her shoulders, moving gently in the evening breeze. One hand rested on the gate, which stood open, completely open, for the first time since she had arrived at his estate.

Devon froze, the nightmare's terror transforming into something else entirely. Not the fear of losing her to force or manipulation, but the fear of losing her to choice. Freedom. He had finally given her what he had taken from her all those months ago.

Unlike in his dreams of Elisabeta's ballroom and dungeon, this choice belonged entirely to Kate.

Devon approached her slowly. He made no attempt to mask his footsteps; she deserved to know he was coming. Kate didn't turn, though the slight stiffening of her shoulders told him she was aware of his presence.

"I wondered when you would wake," she said softly, still gazing out at the road that led away from the estate.

Devon stopped several paces behind her, giving her space. The nightmare's grip finally began to loosen as he heard the warmth in her voice, so different from Elisabeta's cold commands. "I reached for you," he said simply.

Now she turned, and the sight of her face in the soft twilight nearly brought him to his knees. There was a peace in those mossy green eyes that he hadn't seen before, a certainty that both terrified and captivated him. No fear, no coercion, just Kate making her own choice.

"I've been standing here for almost an hour," Kate said, her voice steady.

"Thinking about what it means that this gate is open."

Devon swallowed hard, pushing away the last echoes of Elisabeta's voice. "And what does it mean to you?"

"That you trust me. That you're finally giving me what I asked for from the beginning."

"Freedom," he whispered, the word both beautiful and devastating on his tongue. So different from the twisted choices Elisabeta had forced on him. This was real freedom, freely given.

Kate nodded, her eyes never leaving his. "I thought about walking through. Just… walking away. Calling a taxi, going to the airport, flying back to New York." Her fingers tightened on the gate. "I had it all planned out."

Devon felt something crack inside him, a pain so sharp he almost doubled over. But he remained still, his face carefully composed. He would not manipulate her, not now. Not ever again. He would not become his maker and use the same tools of control Elisabeta had used on him.

"I understand," he managed, though the words felt like glass in his throat.

Kate took a step toward him, then another, moving away from the threshold of freedom. "Do you? Do you understand what I realized standing here?"

Hope, dangerous, fragile hope, flickered in his chest. "Tell me."

"I realized that freedom isn't just about open gates and unlocked doors." She moved closer still, close enough that he could smell her jasmine perfume. "It's about choice. And standing here, knowing I could leave, knowing you would let me go… I finally understood what I truly want."

Devon's hands trembled at his sides. He wanted to reach for her, to pull her against him, but he held back. This moment belonged to her—her choice, her freedom, her decision. "And what do you want, Kate?" His voice was barely audible, even to his own ears.

She smiled then, a small, knowing smile that transformed her face and banished the last shadows of his nightmare. "I want you to meet my parents."

Of all the things she might have said, this was the last thing Devon expected. He blinked, momentarily speechless. "Your… parents?"

Kate laughed, the sound light and uplifting in the evening air. "Yes, Devon. My parents. The people who shaped me into the woman you love."

He gazed down at her, realizing that she was inviting him into her world, her world before Devon Karlov. It hadn't occurred to him before that such a level of inclusion would be possible, but for Kate...

"Meet your family... Kate, are you sure?"

She took a few steps towards him before wrapping her arms around him completely, hooking them under his armpits in a massive, affectionate embrace. Her body pressed fully against his, her face nestled into his chest. It wasn't just a hug, but a declaration of trust and safety found in his arms.

"I can't imagine my life without you in it now," she murmured against his shirt. "I've tried, standing here at this gate, I really tried to picture going back to New York, back to my old life. But I can't even begin to imagine it anymore without you in it. That person doesn't exist. I've changed too much. We've changed too much."

Devon's arms circled Kate, holding her tight against him. The relief of holding her was overwhelming, a physical sensation that coursed through his immortal body like blood. "Your family, your friends... they'll have questions about where you've been, about who I am."

Kate pulled back just enough to look up at him, her fingers now tracing the line of his jaw, a touch so intimate it made him shiver. "We'll figure it out together. But I need this, Devon. I need to try at least to connect these two parts of my life if we're going to have any future together."

Future. Another word that now held new meaning. For centuries, the future had been an endless, monotonous stretch of time. Now, with Kate, every moment held possibility.

"Then yes," he said, bending to press his forehead against hers. "I'll meet your parents. I'll meet anyone you want me to meet."

Kate smiled against his lips. "It won't be easy, you know. My brother is extremely protective, and my father will probably interrogate you about your intentions."

Devon laughed softly. "After facing Aleksander and vampire society, I think I can handle your family."

"Don't be so sure," she teased, rising on her toes to kiss him properly. The kiss deepened, Kate's body melting against his as Devon's arms tightened around her. Here, in the shadow of the open gate, they sealed their new understanding. No longer captor and captive, no longer patron and protégée, but partners choosing each other freely.

When they finally broke apart, a blush creeping into Kate's cheeks, Devon pointed to the gate. "Do you want me to close it?"

Kate stared at it for a moment. "No," she said softly, shaking her head. "Leave it open. I like it that way. Knowing that I chose this."

Devon nodded, understanding the significance of her words. "Where shall we begin? New York?"

"New Jersey, actually. My parents live in Montclair." Kate's eyes sparkled with mischief. "I hope you're ready for suburban family life, Mr Karlov. It's a bit different from your aristocratic vampire existence."

Devon laughed, a genuine sound of joy that surprised even him. "For you, Kate Morgan, I'm ready for anything."

Hand in hand, they walked back toward the house, leaving the gate open behind them—a symbol of the freedom they had both found in choosing each other. As they reached the terrace, Kate turned to him with a sudden seriousness. "There's just one thing."

"What is it?" Devon asked, instantly alert to her change in tone.

"When we're with my family…" She hesitated, choosing her words carefully. "No vampire business. No mentions of your true nature, no midnight feedings, nothing that would reveal what you are. Can you promise me that?"

Devon considered her request. It would be difficult to maintain the illusion of humanity, but for Kate, he would do anything.

"I promise," he said solemnly. "As far as your family is concerned, I'm just a wealthy European art collector who fell hopelessly in love with their daughter."

Kate's smile returned, bright enough to rival the moon above. "Well, that part is true, at least."

She led him inside, already talking about flight arrangements and what to pack, her excitement infectious. Devon followed, listening to her plans with a mixture of trepidation and anticipation.

In all his centuries of existence, he had never met a lover's parents. He had never been introduced as someone's significant other, had never navigated the complex waters of human family dynamics. It was both terrifying and exhilarating at the same time.

As Kate disappeared into the closet to begin packing, Devon stood by the window, gazing out at the open gate in the distance. Whatever came next, meeting Kate's family, navigating her world, facing the inevitable challenges of their unusual relationship, Devon knew that they would face it together. As partners.

And that, Devon realized, was the only freedom that had ever truly mattered.

Chapter 2

Later that night, Devon stood in their large walk-in closet, staring at rows of tailored suits, silk shirts, and handcrafted Italian shoes. For the first time in centuries, he was at a loss for what to wear.

"You look like you're contemplating your own execution," Kate remarked from the doorway, amusement dancing in her eyes.

Devon turned to her, grateful for the interruption. "I've negotiated with kings, dined with dictators, and faced down rival vampires, but somehow the idea of meeting your father has me… unsettled."

Kate crossed the room to stand beside him, her bare feet silent on the carpet. She wore only his dress shirt, the hem skimming her thighs. "The great Devon Karlov, vampire aristocrat, afraid of a retired English professor?"

"Terrified," he admitted, pulling her against him. His voice lowered, a raw honesty coloring his tone. "What does one wear to meet the parents of the woman he abducted and then fell in love with?"

Kate's teasing expression softened at his vulnerable admission. She didn't deny his words, but instead met his honesty with her own. "You wear the face of the man who earned her trust," she said softly. "The man who opened the gate. That's the only one they need to meet." She laughed, and the sound warmed him from within. "And definitely not that," she said, pointing to a formal black suit that would have fit right in at a state dinner. "My dad wears tweed jackets with elbow patches and thinks a tie is formal wear."

Devon's fingers traced idle patterns on her back. "I want to make a good impression."

"Just be yourself," Kate said, then paused. "Well, not your vampire self.

Your charming, art-loving, Kate-adoring self."

"That's the only self that matters anymore," Devon murmured, bending to kiss her neck.

Kate tilted her head, giving him better access. "We need to talk about… practical considerations," she said, her breath catching as his lips found a sensitive spot below her ear.

"Hmm?" Devon was only half listening, distracted by her quickening pulse beneath his mouth.

"Blood," Kate said firmly, though she made no move to pull away. "You'll need to feed before we leave, and then what? We'll be there for at least a week."

Devon straightened, his expression serious. "Already taken care of. Marcus is arranging a local supply to be delivered to our hotel. Medical grade, discreet packaging."

"Hotel?" Kate raised an eyebrow. "I thought we'd stay with my parents. They have a spare room."

Devon tried to mask his alarm, but Kate caught it immediately and burst out laughing. "Your face!" she gasped between fits of giggles. "Don't worry, we're definitely getting a hotel. I wouldn't subject you to my childhood bedroom with its twin bed and my parents down the hall."

Relief washed over him. "I was trying to calculate how I'd explain refusing breakfast every morning without seeming rude."

"You'll still have to navigate some meals," Kate pointed out. "Sunday dinner is non-negotiable in the Morgan household."

Devon nodded, already planning how to move food around his plate without actually consuming any. "I'll manage. I've had centuries of practice appearing human."

Kate rested her hands on his chest. "Thank you for doing this. I know it's not easy for you."

"Nothing about us has been easy," Devon said, capturing her hand and pressing a kiss to her palm. "But everything about us has been worth it."

Kate's eyes darkened deliciously. She rose on her tiptoes, her lips a breath away from his. "We have hours before we need to leave for the airport…"

Devon grinned as he lifted her effortlessly, her legs wrapping around his waist as he carried her toward the bed. "Hours," he agreed, his voice a low rumble against her skin. "Let's make them count."

His mouth captured hers in a kiss that was deep and searching. He laid her on the bed, the fabric of his shirt cool against her skin as he followed her down. Her hands moved from his shoulders to his hair, pulling him closer. The kiss deepened until the world outside the room faded away.

He broke the kiss to trail a path down her neck, his lips and teeth grazing the sensitive skin over her pulse. A shiver wracked her body. "Devon," she breathed, as if speaking his name might save her from his ministrations.

They shed their clothes in a hurried, silent frenzy; zippers and clasps giving way in earnest. In the dim light, Devon's body was a masterpiece of muscle and shadow, ancient and powerful. Kate got up to kneel in front of him as he began to unbutton the shirt she wore—his shirt—his fingers slow and deliberate, revealing her delicate half-moon breasts to his appreciative gaze.

"You are just so beautiful," he murmured, his eyes dark with a hunger that made her feel like the only woman in the world.

"Likewise, Mr Karlov," she whispered, reaching out to trace the lean muscles of his chest before her hand descended low, lower, lower still...

Her eyes drank in his reaction as he shuddered in response to her fingers wrapping with confidence and familiarity around his already stiff length. Her nose nuzzled the base of his neck as she began to stroke leisurely. Devon's hand gravitated south over Kate's breast, brushing her nipple with his knuckles, then her stomach, hip bones, eager to return the favor.

Kate's breath hitched as his fingers reached their final destination, running circles around her clit at a sensual pace. Her eyes closed at the sensation, pressing into Devon to steady herself. Her free hand reached around the back of his neck for support, yet her attention to his own pleasure did not falter. One finger, then two, dipped slowly in and out of her, coating themselves in her silky, wet heat.

She lifted her gaze from the nape of his neck to his eyes, panting now under his handiwork. She guided his other hand to her heart, letting him feel its soft, human rhythm. "This is for you, it's all yours."

That did it. He pushed her back onto the bed and surged over her body like a wave. For the briefest of moments, Devon held himself poised at her entrance, eyes locked with hers, rubbing the head of his cock in sweet agony against her soft, warm center. It was a look of raw, heated need, begging for her surrender. Kate didn't put up a fight; her hips arched upward in encouragement. He was on her, in her, a seamless, urgent thrust that left them both gasping, a single, shared sound of ecstasy.

It was not gentle lovemaking; it was a desperate, primal claiming. A branding and silent vow made in the language of touch, breath and heat. He moved with a frantic rhythm against the quiet of the coming dawn, each thrust deep and sure, erasing the space between them, erasing the doubts and fears that had plagued them.

His hands were tangled in her hair as he tilted her head back. His mouth found hers again, kissing her with a fierce intensity that she matched. It was a kiss that tasted of salt, desire, and the metallic hint of his own inhumanity. Kate's nails raked down his back, not in aggression, but in a desperate attempt to anchor herself to him as he dove into the depths of her, as if she could absorb him into her very soul.

He broke the kiss, pressing his forehead against hers. "Kate," he rasped, the sound giving away a need for her that he couldn't deny. It was the only word he seemed capable of. She could sense his ancient control finally giving way to pure, uninhibited sensations. The civilized veneer stripped away to reveal the powerful, possessive creature beneath. A creature that was entirely, terrifyingly, hers.

Kate felt a familiar craving for the deeper connection they'd shared before. She could see Devon's fangs had already extended slightly in response to his arousal, and the sight sent a thrill through her.

"Devon," she whispered against his lips, her hand sliding to the back of his neck. "I want you to bite me."

His movements stilled, eyes searching hers with careful intensity. "Kate, are you sure? You don't have to—"

"I want to," she interrupted softly. "I've missed feeling that close to you."

Devon's control wavered, his fangs fully extending now. "Tell me where."

Kate tilted her head, exposing the curve of her neck. "Here."

When his fangs pierced her skin, there was a brief, sharp sensation like pressure building and then popping, followed immediately by waves of pleasure that made her gasp and arch against him. Devon groaned against her throat, the taste of her blood and the intimacy of the moment overwhelming him.

"God, Kate," he breathed, his voice rough with emotion and desire.

The connection was electric, tying them together in a way that felt uniquely theirs. Kate felt claimed and cherished, while Devon felt trusted and fully accepted. He drove into her again and again at a relentless pace that was both punishment and praise as he fed from her. She met him thrust for thrust, her body alive and alight in a way she had only ever been with him.

The exquisite friction between their bodies was overwhelming. Kate's inner walls began to tighten around him as she teetered on the edge of all-consuming pleasure. Her breath hitched before spilling out into cries loud enough to wake the dead. Devon chased after her orgasm, filling her with a ragged groan of release. She milked him dry as she clung to him through her quakes, afraid of what would happen if she let go.

Kate's breath came in shuddering waves as Devon delicately licked at the wounds on her neck and held her in his arms. He was still inside her, but the tide of passion had surged and now subsided. Reluctantly, Devon pulled away from her, and she curled against his side, her head on his chest, listening to the silence within.

"If we miss our flight," she murmured, her voice husky with satisfaction, "it will be entirely your fault."

Devon chuckled, the sound a low vibration against her ear. He stroked her hair, his touch infinitely gentle. "I gladly take the blame."

Later, as Kate dozed beside him, Devon found himself watching the gentle rise and fall of her chest. The contrast never failed to move him; her warm humanity against his cold immortality. Her life, so brief and precious, against his endless existence.

These thoughts had occupied him more frequently since their confrontation with Aleksander. The vampire society's disapproval of human-vampire relationships wasn't merely prejudice; it was a practical concern.

Many still adhered to the Pet system, a human companion who primarily served the purpose of providing a willing blood source to their vampire benefactor. Then, of course, humans age. They die. Or they are turned, losing their humanity forever. He pushed the thought away, but it lingered. Someday, he would have to face this choice, but not today.

Today was about Kate and her family, about taking this next step in their relationship. The future, with all its complications, could wait. "You're thinking too loudly," Kate murmured, her voice thick with sleep.

Devon smiled, brushing a strand of hair from her face. "Just contemplating how lucky I am."

"Mmm, nice save," she said, stretching like a cat. "But I know that brooding look. What's really on your mind?"

"Meeting your family," he said, which wasn't entirely a lie. "I'm wondering what they'll make of me."

Kate propped herself up on one elbow, studying his face. "They'll see what I see, a cultured, intelligent man who treats me well and makes me happy."

"A man," Devon repeated. "Not a vampire who kidnapped their daughter."

Kate's expression grew serious. "We agreed not to dwell on how we met. What matters is where we are now." She reached her hand around his neck to cup his head. "And where we're going."

Devon raised his own hand to trace her jawline. "And where are we going, Kate Morgan?"

"Forward," she said simply with a smile. "Together."

The certainty in her voice calmed him. No matter what challenges came next, her family's scrutiny, the vampire society's disapproval, or the basic question of her mortality, they would face them together.

"We should finish packing," Kate said, pulling away from him with some hesitation. "Our flight leaves in a few hours."

Devon watched as she slipped from the bed, admiring the graceful lines of her naked body as she moved across the room. "Private jet," he reminded her. "It leaves when we're ready."

Kate rolled her eyes, but her smile betrayed her. "Of course it does. I keep forgetting I'm dating someone who can casually say things like 'private jet.'"

"Partner," Devon corrected gently. "Not dating. Partners."

Her face warmed with quiet affection. "Partners," she agreed. "Now help your partner pack, or we'll never leave this bedroom."

* * *

A few hours later, they were airborne, the lights of Budapest falling away beneath them. Kate sat across from Devon in the luxurious cabin, a glass of champagne in her hand. "To new beginnings," she said, raising her glass.

Devon touched his glass to hers. "To new beginnings."

Kate took a sip, then set her glass down, her expression turning thoughtful. "We should talk about our cover story. My parents think I've been at an exclusive artist residency in Europe."

"Which isn't entirely untrue," Devon pointed out. "You have been creating art in Europe."

"Yes, but the circumstances were hardly conventional," Kate said dryly. "We need a believable explanation for how we met, how we fell in love, all of it."

Devon leaned forward, giving it some thought. "The gallery opening in Budapest. That part is true. I saw your work, was captivated by it, and by you."

"And then?"

"I invited you to visit my estate, to see my collection." Devon's lips curved in a small smile. "You were impressed, but cautious. We spent time together, discussing art, music, and literature. A whirlwind romance developed."

Kate nodded slowly. "Simple, mostly truthful, and romantic enough. I like it." She paused, considering. "What about your background? They'll want to know about your family, your work."

"I am what I appear to be, a wealthy European art collector with old family money," Devon said. "As for family, they're all deceased. I'm the last of my line."

"That's convenient," Kate said with a wry smile.

"It's also true," Devon reminded her gently. "Everyone I knew in my human life has been dust for centuries."

Sadness crossed Kate's face. She moved from her seat to join him on his side of the cabin, curling against him. "I'm sorry. Sometimes I forget how much loss you've experienced."

Devon wrapped an arm around her shoulders. "It's the nature of immortality. You learn to let go, or you go mad with grief." His tone was distant, and Kate sensed there was more he wasn't saying.

"Is that why vampires keep humans at a distance?"

Devon went quiet for a moment. "In some ways, yes. But it's also about power. The majority of vampires see humans as simply food sources or temporary amusements, not equals." He hesitated. "Then for some, the bond between a maker and their progeny is a form of possession that can be difficult to escape."

"But not you," Kate said, a statement that was also a question.

"Not anymore," Devon admitted, looking at her. "But I can't say I always felt this way. Living for centuries can harden how you see things."

"Until someone shows up to shake things up?" Kate suggested, her eyes teasing.

Devon laughed softly, breaking the tension. "Until a stubborn, talented, impossibly brave artist refuses to be a Pet and demands to be seen as an equal."

She rested her head against his shoulder with a chuckle, her eyes drifting to the window where clouds parted occasionally to reveal the dark landscape below.

After a long moment, Devon reached into the inner pocket of his jacket.

"I have something for you," he said, his voice low. He opened his hand to reveal a delicate, tarnished silver chain, from which hung a single, smooth moonstone. It was milky seemed to glow with a soft, internal light as it rested in his palm.

"It was my mother's, I want you to have it", Devon said, his thumb gliding over the cool surface of the stone.

Kate was speechless. It wasn't just a piece of jewelry; it was part of his history. "Devon," she whispered, her fingers exploring the exquisite gem. "It's beautiful."

She turned around and lifted her hair so he could put it on her. His cool fingers brushed against her neck as he fastened the clasp. The pendant settled against her skin, a comforting weight against her collarbone. It felt like a promise of a shared future, a future he was entrusting to her.

He kissed her neck when he was done. "It suits you," he whispered.

She turned to kiss him on the lips, "Thank you, I love it."

A cloud of worry drifted across her face, Devon noticed. "What are you thinking?"

"About my parents," Kate admitted. "About how to explain my absence, my sudden reappearance with a mysterious European partner." She smiled against his shoulder. "They'll have questions. Lots of questions."

"And we'll answer them as truthfully as we can without revealing what can't be revealed." Devon assured her.

Kate sighed. "I hate lying to them."

"I know." Devon pressed a kiss to the top of her head. "But some truths are too dangerous, for them and for us." The vampire world had strict rules about humans knowing their secrets. Devon was already taking a risk by bringing Kate into his life so completely. Extending that risk to her family was unthinkable.

"Get some rest," he suggested, noticing the fatigue in her eyes. "We have a long journey ahead."

Kate nodded, settling more comfortably against him. "Wake me when we're close to landing?"

"I will," Devon promised.

As Kate fell asleep in his arms, Devon watched the night outside his window. No matter how tricky meeting Kate's parents and feigning human behavior would be, Devon knew one thing for certain: Kate was worth it all. He pressed another gentle kiss to her hair and settled in for the long flight, his mind already rehearsing what he would say to the man who had raised the incredible woman sleeping in his arms.

Chapter 3

The Montclair evening was unusually warm for early Spring, the air smelling of blossoms and freshly cut grass. Devon stood beside Kate outside a modest two-story home with its white clapboard exterior glowing softly in the porch light.

"Home sweet home," Kate said, a mixture of excitement and apprehension in her voice.

Devon took in the details. The garden was well-kept, bursting with flowers. The porch swing moved softly in the breeze. Warm light poured from windows framed by blue shutters. This scene was typically American, completely ordinary, yet entirely new to him. The scent of lives lived and love shared within those walls felt vibrant and real.

"It's lovely," he said, meaning it. There was something deeply appealing about the home's unpretentious warmth.

Kate squeezed his hand. "Ready?"

Devon felt a flutter of something dangerously close to fear. It was the fear of rejection, not for himself, but for her. The fear that they would see the monster he worked so hard to conceal. "As ready as I'll ever be," he replied, adjusting the bottle of wine they'd brought as a gift.

They had barely reached the porch steps when the front door flew open, spilling more light onto the walkway.

"Katie!" A woman in her early sixties rushed forward, arms outstretched. She had Kate's eyes, the same forest green with flecks of gold, though her once-dark hair was now streaked with silver.

"Mom," Kate breathed, releasing Devon's hand to embrace her mother. The two women held each other tightly, and Devon's heightened senses could detect the faint scent of salt from tears.

"Let me look at you," Eleanor Morgan said, pulling back to cup her daughter's face. "You look… different. Radiant."

Kate smiled, wiping away a tear. "I've missed you so much."

"Then perhaps you should have called more often," came a deeper voice from the doorway. A tall man with a well-trimmed beard and wire-rimmed glasses stood watching them, his posture straight despite his age. Richard Morgan's expression was a careful mixture of joy and reservation.

"Dad," Kate said, moving to embrace him. The man's reserve melted as he wrapped his arms around his daughter, closing his eyes briefly.

"Welcome home, sweetheart," he murmured.

Devon remained on the walkway, giving the family their moment. He was very aware of his outsider status, not just as Kate's new partner, but as a being fundamentally different from these humans with their warm embraces and loud, beating hearts.

Eleanor's gaze shifted to him, curious and assessing. "And you must be Devon."

Devon stepped forward, extending his hand with a practiced smile. "Devon Karlov. It's a pleasure to meet you, Mrs Morgan."

"Eleanor, please," she said, taking his hand. If she noticed its unnatural coolness, she gave no indication.

Richard stepped forward and offered his hand to Devon. "Richard Morgan. Welcome to our home, Mr Karlov."

"Devon, please," he replied, shaking the older man's hand firmly but with immense control. Human bones were so fragile.

"Well, don't keep them standing on the porch, Richard," Eleanor chided, ushering them inside. "Come in, come in. Dinner's almost ready."

The interior of the Morgan home was as warm and inviting as its exterior suggested. Bookshelves lined the living room walls, interspersed with framed family photographs and Kate's artwork from various stages of her development.

"Your home is beautiful," Devon said, genuinely impressed by the sense of history and belonging that filled the space.

"Thank you," Eleanor replied. "We've been here since Kate was five. Couldn't bear to leave after the kids grew up, too many memories."

"Kids?" Devon inquired, though he knew from Kate that she had a brother.

"Jamie will be joining us for dinner," Richard explained, taking a seat in a well-worn leather armchair. "He lives in the city but comes back most weekends."

"He's dying to meet you," Eleanor added with a smile that suggested Kate's brother might have other motivations beyond simple curiosity.

Kate shot Devon an apologetic look. "Jamie's a bit protective."

"As older brothers should be," Richard said mildly, though his eyes were sharp as they assessed Devon. "Especially when their sisters disappear to Europe for months."

The air in the room suddenly felt tense. Devon could hear Kate's heartbeat accelerate slightly. "Dad, we talked about this," she said uncomfortably. "The residency was intensive. I was creating, exhibiting—"

"And falling in love, apparently," Eleanor chipped in, her tone softening the observation. "Which is wonderful, of course. We just wish we'd been more… included."

Devon stepped in smoothly. "The fault is entirely mine," he said. "I'm afraid I've been rather selfish with Kate's time. When you see the work she's created these past months, I think you'll understand why the art world in Budapest was so captivated by her."

Richard's expression remained unconvinced, but Eleanor seemed to warm slightly at Devon's words. "Well, you're both here now," she said, rising. "And I hope you'll be comfortable at your hotel. Though you know you're always welcome to stay here, Katie."

"The hotel is perfect, Mom," Kate assured her. "It's close by, and Devon has some work calls to manage with the time difference."

Devon nodded, grateful for Kate's smooth handling of the excuse. The real reason, his need for privacy to consume the blood Marcus had arranged to be delivered, was not something her parents could ever know.

"Richard, why don't you offer our guests a drink while I finish up in the kitchen?" Eleanor suggested.

"Of course," Richard said, standing. "What can I get you? Wine? Beer? Something stronger?"

"Wine would be lovely," Kate said. "Devon?"

"The same, thank you," Devon replied, though he would only pretend to sip it. Human food and drink held no appeal for him, but appearances had to be maintained.

As Richard moved to the small bar cart in the corner, the front door opened again, and a tall man with Kate's dark hair and her father's build stepped into the foyer. "Am I late?" he called, shrugging off his jacket.

"Jamie!" Kate exclaimed, rushing to embrace her brother.

Jamie Morgan hugged his sister tightly, lifting her slightly off the ground. "There's my favorite artist," he said, setting her down. "Let me look at you. Europe agrees with you, sis."

"I've missed you," Kate said, her smile genuine.

Jamie's gaze shifted to Devon, his expression cooling noticeably. "And this must be the mysterious European boyfriend."

"Partner," Kate corrected, returning to Devon's side. "Jamie, this is Devon Karlov. Devon, my brother Jamie."

Devon extended his hand. "A pleasure to meet you, Jamie."

Jamie's handshake was firmer than necessary, a subtle test of strength that Devon could have easily won but deliberately didn't. "Likewise," Jamie said, though his tone suggested otherwise. "So, art collector, right? That's what Kate said."

"Among other interests," Devon replied smoothly. "But art is my passion."

"Dinner's ready," Eleanor said. "Shall we move to the dining room?" The dining room continued the home's theme of comfortable elegance with a polished oak table set with what Devon guessed was the family's best china.

"It looks wonderful, Mom," Kate said, taking her seat. Devon sat beside her, acutely aware of the challenge ahead. He would need to move food around his plate convincingly, take occasional pretend sips of wine, and maintain the illusion of humanity throughout the meal. Centuries of practice made the deception effortless.

"So, Devon," Richard began as Eleanor served a garden salad, "Kate tells us you're Hungarian?"

"My family has roots there, yes," Devon replied. "Though I've lived throughout Europe."

"And what brought you to Budapest specifically?" Richard continued, his tone casual, but his eyes sharp.

"The art scene, primarily," Devon said. "Budapest has experienced a renaissance in contemporary art over the past decade. I wanted to be part of it."

"Lucky for you that Kate's residency happened to be there," Jamie commented, spearing a cherry tomato with unnecessary force.

Devon nodded and looked directly at the young man. "When I saw Kate's work at the gallery opening, I knew I had to meet her. What followed was… unexpected, but not unwelcome."

The sincerity of the moment seemed to ease some of the tension in the room. Even Jamie's posture relaxed slightly.

"Katie's always painted from the heart," Eleanor said proudly. "Even as a child. So, Katie," Eleanor said as she served dessert, "will you be visiting your old studio while you're here? Zoe's been asking about you."

"Definitely," Kate replied. "I want to show Devon my old neighborhood, maybe visit a few galleries."

"I'm looking forward to seeing where Kate lived and worked," Devon added. "To better understand her artistic journey."

Jamie snorted softly. "Artistic journey. Right."

"Jamie," Richard warned.

"No, it's fine," Jamie said, setting down his fork. "I just find it interesting that my sister disappears to Europe for a 'residency,' barely calls home, then shows up with a wealthy European boyfriend—"

"Partner," Kate corrected again, her voice tight.

"—partner, whatever, who talks about art like he's reading from a catalog." Jamie leaned forward. "What's the real story here? Because something doesn't add up."

Devon felt Kate tense beside him, her heart beating double time. This was dangerous territory.

"The real story," Devon said calmly, "is exactly what we've told you. Kate and I met at her exhibition. The rest developed naturally."

"Naturally," Jamie repeated skeptically. "And the fact that you're clearly wealthy had nothing to do with it?"

"Jamie!" Eleanor exclaimed.

Kate stood abruptly, her chair scraping against the hardwood floor. "That's enough," she said, her voice shaking with anger. "I didn't come home to be insulted or to have Devon insulted. If you can't be civil, we'll leave."

Devon placed a gentle hand on her arm. "Kate, it's all right. Your brother is concerned for you. I respect that."

"Concern doesn't excuse rudeness," Kate insisted, but she sat back down.

An uncomfortable silence fell over the table. Richard cleared his throat.

"Maybe we should move to the living room for coffee," he suggested. "Jamie, a word in the kitchen, please."

As Richard and Jamie disappeared into the kitchen, Eleanor began gathering dessert plates, waving away Kate's offer to help.

"I'm so sorry about that," Kate whispered to Devon when they were momentarily alone. "Jamie's always been overprotective, but this is ridiculous."

"He loves you," Devon said simply. "He sees a stranger who's suddenly become important in your life, and he's suspicious. It's natural."

"It's annoying," Kate muttered.

Devon smiled and brushed a strand of hair from her face. "Give him time. He'll come around."

Eleanor served coffee in the living room as Richard and Jamie rejoined them, Jamie looking suitably chastened. The conversation shifted to safer topics, including family updates and plans for their visit.

Devon found himself genuinely enjoying the glimpse into Kate's family life. Despite initial tensions, there was a warmth and love in the Morgan household that reminded him of what he'd lost so long ago.

"We should probably head back to the hotel," Kate said eventually, stifling a yawn. "Jet lag is catching up with me."

"Of course," Eleanor said, rising. "But you'll come for Sunday dinner?

Jamie will be here again, and he'll be on his best behavior." She shot her son a pointed look.

"Scout's honor," Jamie said, raising his hand in a mock salute.

"We'd be delighted," Devon replied before Kate could answer. He wanted, needed, this connection with her family to work, for her sake.

As they gathered their coats and prepared to leave, Jamie cleared his throat. "Devon, can I talk to you for a second? Outside, maybe?"

Kate tensed beside Devon, clearly expecting another confrontation. Devon placed a reassuring hand on her arm. "Of course."

Devon followed Jamie out onto the front porch, its light casting long shadows across the lawn. Jamie leaned against the porch railing, his hands shoved deep in his pockets. For a moment, he looked younger than his thirty-two years, more like the protective big brother he'd always been than the suspicious interrogator from dinner.

"I owe you an apology," Jamie said finally, his voice quiet in the evening air. "What I said in there, the way I acted, it was out of line."

Devon remained silent, sensing there was more Jamie needed to say.

"Dad read me the riot act in the kitchen," Jamie continued with a rueful smile. "Reminded me that Kate's happiness should matter more than my paranoia." He paused, studying Devon's face in the dim light. "My behaviour tonight wasn't really about you."

"No?" Devon asked gently.

Jamie shook his head, his jaw tightening with old anger. "Kate told you about her ex, Jason, didn't she?"

Devon nodded. "She did."

"Then you know what that bastard put her through," Jamie said, his voice growing harder. "The way he stole her artistic concepts and passed them as his own, destroyed her confidence."

Devon felt the familiar rage stir in his chest at the mention of Kate's ex, the same fury he'd felt when she'd first told him the story. "Yes, I know."

"What Kate probably didn't tell you," Jamie continued, his voice heavy with guilt, "is that I introduced them. Jason was one of my friends at the time. Seemed like a good guy, stable. I thought he'd be perfect for Kate." His voice cracked slightly. "I practically pushed them together.'"

The weight of Jamie's guilt felt almost physical in the cool night air. Devon now understood why Kate's brother had been so hostile; it wasn't just protectiveness, but the fear of making the same mistake twice.

"I should have seen the signs when Kate started pulling away from us. Should have asked more questions, pushed harder when she made excuses not to visit."

Devon felt a surge of empathy. "You blame yourself for not protecting her."

"I was supposed to be her big brother," Jamie said, his voice barely above a whisper.

"And now you see another charming man who's swept her off her feet," Devon said quietly, the pieces falling into place.

Jamie nodded, meeting Devon's eyes directly. "Wealthy, charming, older man from a different world who appeared in her life and changed everything? Yeah, it rang every alarm bell I had." He paused. "But watching you two tonight, seeing how you look at her, how you let her take the lead in conversations about her own life… I was wrong. You're nothing like Jason."

Devon felt some of his tension ease. "Thank you for recognizing that. Kate's family is important to her; therefore, they're important to me."

Jamie looked down at his shoes. "I'm sorry for questioning your motives and making you feel unwelcome. It wasn't fair to you, and it wasn't what Kate needed."

Devon extended his hand. "Apology accepted. And Jamie? I understand why you were protective. After what happened with Jason… I respect that you're looking out for her."

Before either could say more, the front door opened and Kate appeared.

"Are you two plotting out there?" she asked, though her tone was light. "Mom's getting worried you're going to start throwing punches."

"Just getting to know each other," Jamie said easily, though his eyes held a new warmth when he looked at Devon. "Turns out we're both looking out for the same person."

As they said their final goodbyes, Eleanor hugged Kate tightly and even gave Devon a brief embrace, Richard shook Devon's hand with more warmth than earlier, and Jamie managed a genuine smile and a firm handshake.

"Welcome to the family, Devon," he said quietly. "Take care of her."

"Always," Devon replied, meaning it with every fiber of his being.

Kate let out a long breath as they drove away from the Morgan home. "Well, that went better than expected. What did you and Jamie talk about out there? You both seemed… different when you came back in."

Devon reached for her hand, squeezing gently, but his eyes flicked to the rearview mirror. A dark sedan had been following them since they left Kate's parents' house, maintaining a careful distance, but making every turn they made.

"Just… getting to know each other," he said, his voice slightly distracted. "He's a good man, Kate. He loves you very much."

"He does," Kate agreed, settling back in her seat. "He can be overprotective sometimes, but after everything with Jason…" She trailed off, then looked at Devon curiously. "He didn't give you the whole 'hurt my sister and I'll kill you' speech, did he?"

Devon smiled, though his attention remained split between Kate and the persistent vehicle behind them. "Something like that. But I understand where it comes from."

Kate sighed. "I know he blames himself for introducing me to Jason. I've tried to tell him it wasn't his fault, but…"

"Guilt is a powerful thing," Devon said softly, checking the mirror again. The sedan was still there, its headlights steady in the darkness. His vampire senses picked up something else, a familiar scent on the wind, ancient and dangerous.

Kate squeezed his hand. "Thank you for being patient with him. I know he was difficult."

"He was protecting someone he loves," Devon said, bringing her hand to his lips while his eyes tracked the sedan's movements. "I can hardly fault him for that."

Kate turned to look out the back window, frowning. "Devon, is that car following us?"

Devon's hands tightened slightly on the steering wheel. "Why do you ask?"

"It's been behind us since we left my parents' house. Same distance, every turn." Kate's voice carried a note of unease. "That's not normal, is it?"

Devon forced his voice to remain calm. "It's probably just someone heading in the same direction."

But even as he said it, he was calculating alternate routes to the hotel, his mind automatically shifting into the protective mode that had kept him alive for centuries.

"Maybe," Kate said, but she didn't sound convinced. She studied Devon's profile in the dim light from the dashboard. "You seem tense."

"Just tired from the evening," he replied, but his jaw was tight with barely controlled tension.

The sedan followed them for another three miles before finally turning off onto a side street. Devon didn't relax until they were safely in the hotel parking garage, his heightened awareness scanning for any lingering threats.

As they walked toward the elevator, Kate touched his arm. "Devon, what aren't you telling me?"

He looked at her—beautiful, trusting, unaware of the dangers that might be circling them—and felt the familiar weight of protecting her from his world.

"Nothing's wrong," he said, forcing a smile. "Just adjusting to being back in the city."

But as the elevator doors closed, Devon's mind was already working, planning extra security measures and considering whether they should cut their New York visit short. The past was reaching for them, and he would do whatever it took to keep Kate safe.

Even if it meant keeping secrets of his own.

Chapter 4

Kate felt strange being back in New York for the first few days; it was all an odd blend of the familiar and the foreign to her now. After the tense dinner with her parents, Kate had expected to feel out of kilter. Instead, she found a quiet, domestic rhythm with Devon in their luxurious hotel suite.

He was a being of stillness and shadow until sunset, and she, by necessity, was beginning to adapt. Her sleep schedule shifted, her days becoming a quiet, solitary prelude to the vibrant life they lived after the city lights blinked on.

She spent the daylight hours falling in love with her city all over again, seeing it through new, bittersweet eyes. She explored Soho on foot, sketchbook in hand, capturing intricate details of cast-iron architecture she'd never had the patience to notice before.

Back in the hotel room, as night arrived, the air in the suite shifted. The dormant stillness Devon held during the day dissolved, and he was simply… present. Kate was reading on the sofa when he came out of the bedroom, already dressed for the evening. His eyes sparkled with a playful excitement she hadn't noticed before. It was a sharp contrast to the serious attitude he had during their visit to her family home.

"I have a surprise for you," he said. His voice was a low, smooth rumble that still made her heart race. "I hope you'll indulge me."

Kate closed her book, a smile playing on her lips. "Is this another five-star restaurant where I eat seven courses of things I can't pronounce while you drink whiskey-colored blood and look broodingly handsome?

He chuckled, a rich, genuine sound. "Something better," he promised, taking her hand and pulling her to her feet. "Something for us."

A town car was waiting, its engine a soft purr in the evening air. It didn't take them to a familiar haunt downtown, but to a sleek, modern glass tower in Tribeca that pierced the sky, overlooking the Hudson River. Devon led her into the silent, marble-clad lobby and used a private, unmarked key for the elevator.

"A friend's place?" Kate asked, her curiosity piqued.

"Not exactly," Devon said, tracing circles on the back of her hand with his thumb. When the elevator opened, they were greeted by a large, open, and beautiful apartment with concrete floors. Floor-to-ceiling windows wrapped around the entire living area, offering a stunning, 180-degree panorama of the glittering Manhattan skyline and the dark, shimmering ribbon of the river.

Kate's breath caught in her throat. She let go of Devon's hand and walked slowly into the center of the vast room, turning in a slow circle, trying to take it all in. "Devon, what is this?" she finally asked, her voice a whisper that was easily lost in the empty space.

"I've been thinking," he began, his voice soft as he came to stand beside her, his presence a warm anchor in the cool, empty room. "About what you said. About New York being where you found yourself, where you became an artist. About your friends, your family, your life here."

He gestured to the empty space around them, a sweep of his hand that encompassed the entire city beyond the glass. "My world has been my own for centuries. My estate in Budapest… it's a fortress, built for solitude and defense. It is a reflection of a long, lonely life. That is not a life I want for you. Or for us."

He took her hands, his gaze intense and achingly sincere. "I don't want you to lose the things you love because of me. I don't want you to sacrifice your world for mine. I want us to build one together, a place that belongs to both of us."

Kate's heart swelled, a lump forming in her throat. This was more than she had ever allowed herself to hope for.

"We can split our time," he continued, his words tumbling out with an earnestness that was absolutely adorable. "Budapest, New York. Wherever you need to be for your work." He pointed toward a large, separate room with a wall of north-facing windows. "Your studio could go there. The security is impeccable, and the windows have blackout technology that would allow me to… adjust to a more human schedule if needed. It's close to your friends, galleries, and the city."

He finally turned to her, and for the first time, she saw vulnerability in his ancient eyes, a fear of rejection that was so deeply human it made her ache. "It's nothing like my home. It's modern, it's… stark. But it could be ours. If you like it."

"Like it?" she finally whispered, her voice thick with unshed tears. "Devon, it's… perfect." She stepped towards him and hugged him fiercely, a wave of physical relief washing over him. "It's not just a space. It's a home."

"It's our home," he replied, his voice muffled in her hair.

They spent the next hour exploring the empty apartment like children, their voices echoing in the vast space. They planned where the sofa would go, where they would hang the art from Devon's private collection.

"I need to see the bathroom," Kate said suddenly, her eyes bright with glee. "I need to know if the bathtub is big enough for both of us."

Devon laughed, a rich sound that filled the empty space. "Go explore. I'll be right here."

Kate disappeared down the hallway, her footsteps echoing on the polished concrete floors. Devon could hear her squeals of delight as she discovered the master bathroom's features, the oversized soaking tub, the rainfall shower, and the heated floors.

Alone in the main living area, Devon pulled out his phone to check his secure messages. A new one had arrived from his vampire ally, Antoine.

She is on the move. Will send details tomorrow.

Devon frowned, a flicker of unease stirring in his chest. Antoine was not prone to vagueness or unnecessary drama. If he was sending cryptic warnings, it meant something significant was happening in the vampire world. Something that could affect Devon directly.

He filed the message away to deal with later, his attention drawn back to Kate's voice echoing from the bathroom.

"Devon! You have to see this tub! It's practically a swimming pool!"

Devon smiled despite the lingering unease from Antoine's message. Whatever was happening in his world, whatever threats lay in the shadows, they could wait. Tonight was for Kate, their future, and the home they were creating together.

Chapter 5

The call came at three in the afternoon, just as Kate finished arranging the last of their belongings in the Tribeca apartment. Devon was still in his daylight sleep, his form perfectly still beneath the blackout curtains.

"Kate Morgan?" The voice was crisp, professional.

"Speaking."

"This is Miranda Chen from White Space Gallery in Chelsea. I have an unusual proposition. We had a last-minute cancellation for this weekend. Would you be interested in a pop-up exhibition? This Saturday night?"

Kate's heart skipped. White Space was influential, known for launching careers. "This Saturday? As in, three days from now?"

"I know it's insane, but that's the art world. The space is prepped, and we have the mailing list. We just need art. Good art. David at the Art Students League says you've been working on something new recently."

Kate glanced toward the bedroom where Devon slept, thinking of the canvases she'd completed at his estate. "How many pieces would you need?"

"Twelve to fifteen would be ideal."

Kate mentally catalogued her work. She had enough pieces, and with three days, she could complete a few more. "Yes," she heard herself say. "I can do that.

That afternoon, she began the task of pulling canvases from their careful wrapping, studying the work she'd created in Devon's world with new eyes. The paintings were good, better than good. They pulsed with an emotional intensity she'd never achieved before, each one a meditation on transformation, desire, and the complex journey of self-discovery.

When Devon woke at sunset, he found her surrounded by her art, the living room transformed into an impromptu studio.

"What's all this?" he asked, his voice still rough with sleep.

Kate looked up from where she was touching up a corner of one painting. "I got a call today. There's a gallery in Chelsea, they want to give me a show. This Saturday."

Devon moved through the paintings, studying each piece. Kate watched nervously as his eyes took in the work born from their relationship, from the intensity of her time in captivity at his estate.

"They're extraordinary," he said finally.

"You don't mind that they're about… us?"

"Kate, these are your experiences, your emotions, your art. They belong to you completely." He paused. "Will you be ready?"

Kate nodded, feeling some of her anxiety ease. "I think so. Will you come? To the opening?"

"Wild horses couldn't keep me away," Devon said, then paused with a slight smile. "Though I should probably prepare myself for my first opening as the artist's partner. It's been a while since I've attended one where I had such a personal investment in the work."

* * *

Saturday evening arrived soon enough. White Space Gallery took up the ground floor of a converted warehouse in Chelsea, its industrial bones softened by careful lighting and polished concrete floors. Miranda Chen met Kate at the door. She was a petite woman in her forties with silver-streaked black hair and a sharp, assessing gaze.

"Kate! The installation looks incredible. Come see."

Kate's paintings hung throughout the space, each one carefully lit and positioned to create a narrative flow. The transformation was breathtaking.

"The response has been incredible," Miranda continued. "We sent the announcement out yesterday, and we're expecting over two hundred people tonight. The Times is sending a reviewer, and I've heard from several established collectors."

Walking through the gallery, Kate stared in wonder at her work in this professional context. Pieces that had been created in the privacy of Devon's estate now commanded attention in one of Chelsea's most respected galleries.

"Are you nervous?" Miranda asked, noticing Kate's quiet intensity.

"Terrified," Kate admitted. "This is all happening so fast."

"The best opportunities usually do," Miranda said with a knowing smile. "Trust your work, Kate. It speaks for itself."

Devon arrived right at seven, just as the first guests were coming in. Kate spotted him immediately. He moved through the crowd with a calm confidence that made him stand out, even if no one else seemed to notice. He wore a well-fitted charcoal suit with a slight shine, and his dark hair was swept back. He looked every bit the polished European art collector he was pretending to be.

Their eyes met across the room, and he gave her a small, reassuring smile before blending back into the crowd. Kate understood that tonight, she needed to be the artist and the focus of attention. He would support her from the sidelines.

The opening night crowd was a mix of serious collectors, art world insiders, curious locals, and the fashionably dressed who attended openings more for the social aspect than the art. Kate found herself swept into conversation after conversation, explaining her work, discussing her process, fielding questions about her inspiration.

Devon appeared at her side as the crowd began to thin slightly. "How are you feeling?" he asked quietly.

"Like I'm living someone else's life," Kate admitted. "This is incredible, Devon. People are actually investing in my work.

"I'm not surprised," Devon said, his voice warm with pride. "Your work is incredible, Kate. You've found your voice as an artist."

"I couldn't have done this without you," she said softly. "The time at your estate, the space to create without worrying about everyday concerns, it gave me the freedom to explore in ways I never could before."

Devon's expression grew serious. "The talent was always there, Kate. I simply provided the environment for it to flourish."

The opening was everything Kate had dreamed of. Critics, collectors, and art lovers moved through the space, their conversations animated as they discussed her work. Several red dots appeared next to paintings, sales that would change her financial situation dramatically.

"Kate?"

She turned towards the familiar voice and her stomach dropped into a deep, bottomless pit. Her ex-boyfriend stood behind her, his smile sharp and predatory. He looked successful in an expensive suit, with a confident posture and the kind of polish that came with money and recognition.

"Jason." Kate's voice was carefully neutral. "What are you doing here?"

"Supporting the arts, of course." His eyes swept over her paintings with a condescending gaze. "Quite the career resurrection you've managed. Though I have to say, I'm surprised to see you showing again after... well, after everything."

Kate felt Devon's presence before she saw him, the slight shift in the air that meant he was near. His hand found the small of her back, a gesture of support and possession.

"Devon Karlov," he said smoothly, extending his hand to Jason. "You must be a friend of Kate's."

Jason's smile faltered slightly as he took in Devon's expensive clothes, his confident bearing, the way Kate unconsciously leaned into his touch. "Jason Reeves. I'm an artist as well. Kate and I have... history."

"How nice," Devon said, his tone polite but cold.

"Yes, we were quite close," Jason continued, his eyes fixed on Kate. "I helped launch her career, actually. Gave her some of her best ideas."

Kate felt her jaw clench. "That's not how I remember it."

"Memory can be so subjective," Jason said with a laugh that didn't reach his eyes. "Especially when success goes to someone's head."

The conversation was drawing attention from nearby guests. Kate could feel eyes turning toward them, sensing drama.

"Perhaps we should continue this somewhere more private," Devon suggested, his voice carrying a subtle threat.

"Actually, that's a good idea," Kate said, surprising them both. "Jason, let's talk. Over here."

She led him to a quieter corner of the gallery, away from the crowd. Devon followed at a discrete distance, close enough to intervene if needed but far enough to let Kate handle this herself.

"What do you want, Jason?" Kate asked once they were alone.

"Want?" Jason's mask slipped, revealing the anger beneath. "I want to know how you managed this. Two years ago, you couldn't sell a painting to save your life. Now you're showing in Chelsea with some European sugar daddy bankrolling your career?"

"Devon isn't bankrolling anything," Kate said firmly. "These paintings are mine. My work, my vision, my success."

"Your success?" Jason laughed bitterly. "Kate, we both know you were nothing before me. I gave you everything: Connections, concepts, and confidence. And how did you repay me? By running away the moment things got difficult."

"Difficult?" Kate's voice rose slightly. "You mean when I found out you'd been presenting my work as your own? When I found out you'd been stealing my ideas for months?"

"We were partners," Jason hissed. "What's yours was mine, what's mine was yours. That's how relationships work."

"That's how theft works," Kate shot back. "And we were never partners, Jason. You were a parasite."

Jason's face darkened. "Careful, Kate. You wouldn't want people to know the truth about your little European adventure, would you?"

Kate felt a chill of fear, but she stood her ground. "You don't know anything about my life."

"Don't I?" Jason stepped closer, his voice dropping to a whisper. "Mysterious wealthy European, no clear profession, keeps you isolated from friends and family for months? Sounds suspicious, doesn't it? Sounds like you just traded one controlling relationship for another."

"You're wrong," Kate said, but she could feel doubt creeping in.

"Am I? Look around, Kate. This gallery, this opening, none of this is really yours, is it? It's all his. And when he gets bored of playing patron to his little pet artist, where will you be?"

The word 'pet' hit Kate like a physical blow, bringing back memories she'd tried to bury. For a moment, she was back in Devon's estate, feeling helpless and controlled.

Then she remembered who she was now. What she'd become.

"You're right about one thing, Jason," she said, her voice steady and strong. "I was nothing before. But not because I didn't have talent or vision. I was nothing because I let people like you convince me I was worthless."

She stepped closer to him, her eyes blazing. "But I'm not that person anymore. I know my worth now, and it has nothing to do with you or anyone else's opinion of me. These paintings? This success? I earned it. Every brushstroke, every moment of doubt, every breakthrough, that's mine."

Jason's confident mask was cracking. "Kate—"

"No," she cut him off. "You had your chance to speak. You stole from me, lied to me, tried to destroy my confidence so I'd be dependent on you. But I survived you, Jason, and I thrived without you." She looked him up and down with obvious disdain. "Now, if you'll excuse me, I have a career to get back to. One that has nothing to do with you."

Kate turned to walk away, but Jason grabbed her arm. "You think you can just walk away from me? After everything I—"

"Is there a problem here?"

Devon's voice was soft, but there was something in it that made Jason immediately release Kate's arm. The vampire stood behind them, his presence suddenly menacing despite his polite expression.

"No problem," Kate said firmly. "Jason was just leaving."

Jason looked between Kate and Devon, seeing something in the other man's eyes that made him take a step back. "Enjoy it while it lasts," he muttered, but the fight had gone out of him.

Kate stood firmly in her own inner strength. "Goodbye, Jason."

They watched him leave, his shoulders hunched in defeat.

"Are you all right?" Devon asked softly.

"That was intense," Kate admitted, a bit shaken from the unexpected visitor. "But I'm OK. Great, even."

As they returned to the gallery opening, Kate felt lighter than she had in years. She had confronted her past and emerged stronger. Whatever challenges lay ahead, she could handle them. She was no longer the woman who could be broken by men like Jason Reeves. She was Kate Morgan, and she was exactly where she belonged.

Chapter 6

For three nights, Kate and Devon began building a life in the empty spaces of their new Tribeca apartment. They ordered furniture, made plans, and fell into a rhythm that was theirs alone. Tonight, however, they were venturing out, leaving their serene sanctuary for the vibrant chaos of Kate's past.

"Are you sure you're ready for this?" Kate asked, a teasing smile on her lips as she adjusted the strap on her boot. "My friends can be… a lot."

Devon, who had been watching her from an armchair they'd had delivered that afternoon, rose and came to stand behind her, his hands resting on her waist. "I think I can handle a gathering of Brooklyn artists," he murmured, his lips brushing her ear. He met her eyes in the reflection from the vast window. "I want to see this part of your life, Kate. The world you built before me."

The sincerity in his voice warmed her. This was what partnership felt like, not just sharing a space, but sharing a history. Their driver navigated the traffic with practiced ease, leaving the polished streets of Tribeca for the grittier, more vibrant avenues of Bushwick, Brooklyn.

"This is it," Kate said as they pulled up to a converted warehouse building. "Home sweet home. Well, former home."

The building was industrial chic with all exposed brick and large windows, a steel door at the entrance. A far cry from Devon's centuries-old estate, and even from their sleek new apartment, but it had a character and authenticity that Kate had missed.

"Zoe's probably got half the art scene here to welcome me back," she said, punching a code into the keypad beside the door. "She's not exactly subtle."

The door buzzed open, revealing a freight elevator with metal grating. Kate stepped in confidently, and Devon followed. He noticed how relaxed she looked in this place, so different from her initial unease at his estate. The elevator opened into a large loft with high ceilings and an open floor plan divided by carefully arranged furniture. Music flowed through the space, and the air was filled with the smell of incense, paint, and people.

"KATE!" A chorus of voices erupted as heads turned toward the elevator.

A whirlwind with purple hair and multiple piercings reached them first, enveloping Kate in a fierce hug. "You absolute ghost! Months of radio silence and then 'Hey Zoe, coming to town with my European boyfriend, make the place presentable'?"

"Partner," Kate corrected automatically, returning the hug with equal enthusiasm. "And I called more than that."

"Barely," Zoe retorted, pulling back to examine her friend. "Look at you! All glowy and European. Budapest agreed with you." Her gaze shifted to Devon, eyes widening appreciatively. "And this must be the mysterious art collector who swept you off your feet."

Devon extended his hand. "Devon Karlov. You must be Zoe. Kate's told me so much about you."

Zoe bypassed his hand entirely, pulling him into a quick, unexpected hug. "We don't do handshakes here, Devon. Welcome to the real world."

Before Devon could respond, a crowd of Kate's friends surrounded her at once, giving her fierce hugs and asking endless questions. Devon observed the interactions with interest. These were Kate's people, fellow artists, gallery assistants, creative souls who had shared her life before him. Devon watched Kate move through the room. She caught his eye occasionally, sending him reassuring smiles, but she was clearly enjoying the reunion with her friends.

Eventually, she made her way back to him, slipping her arm through his. "Sorry about that. Everyone's been saving up months of gossip."

"Don't apologize," Devon said. "It's wonderful to see you in your element."

Kate looked up at him, her expression softening. "Are you okay? I know this isn't exactly your scene."

Devon smiled warmly. "I'm enjoying seeing this part of your life."

"Well, come on then," Kate said, tugging him toward a different group. "There are people you should meet."

The next hour passed in a blur of introductions. Devon met gallery owners who had given Kate her first shows, fellow artists who had shared studio space with her, critics who had championed her work. He observed the easy camaraderie, the inside jokes, the shared history that connected Kate to these people.

"There you are!" Zoe's bounced over to them. "Stop hogging the European art god, Kate. Some of us have questions."

Kate laughed. "Be nice, Zo. Devon's not on trial here."

"Of course he is," Zoe said cheerfully, linking her arm through Devon's. "That's what happens when you date—"

"Partner with," Kate corrected.

"—partner with our beloved Kate. Now come on, Devon. Tell us how you really met. The Budapest gallery story is so boring."

Devon allowed himself to be led back to the main gathering area, where a group had assembled on mismatched furniture around a coffee table laden with drinks and snacks. "The truth is exactly as boring as Kate has told you," Devon said, taking a seat beside Kate on a worn leather sofa. "I attended her exhibition, was captivated by her work, and arranged to meet her."

"And then swept her off to your castle?" a woman with elaborate tattoos covering both arms asked.

"Estate," Devon corrected smoothly. "And the invitation was professional, initially. I wanted to show Kate my collection and discuss her artistic vision."

"But it didn't stay professional," Zoe prompted, leaning forward eagerly.

Kate rolled her eyes. "Seriously, Zo? Are we in high school?"

As the evening went on, Devon saw Kate becoming quiet and more observant. She engaged with her friends, but there was a different look in her eyes. As if she were viewing them from a new angle. Around midnight, the group started to break up. Friends hugged Kate goodbye, extracted promises of coffee dates and gallery visits during her stay, and filtered out of the loft until only Kate, Devon, and Zoe remained.

"You're welcome to crash here," Zoe offered, beginning to clear away empty bottles and glasses. "Your old room is basically a storage closet now, but the sofa pulls out."

"Thanks, but we have our own place now," Kate said, helping with the cleanup.

Zoe nodded, then fixed Devon with a direct look. "So, Devon. Serious question time."

Devon raised an eyebrow, waiting. "Are you good to her? Really good to her?" Zoe asked, all traces of her earlier playfulness gone. "Because Kate's special. She deserves someone who gets that."

Devon met her gaze steadily. "I am fully aware of how extraordinary Kate is," he said quietly. "And I strive every day to be worthy of her choice to be with me."

Zoe studied him for a long moment, then nodded, apparently satisfied. "Good answer. You pass. For now."

Kate rolled her eyes, but Devon could see she was touched by her friend's protectiveness.

"We should go," Kate said, gathering her jacket. "The car's waiting downstairs."

Zoe hugged Kate tightly. "Don't be a stranger this time, okay? New York misses you."

"I won't," Kate promised. "See you tomorrow."

In the elevator descending to the street, Kate leaned against Devon with a sigh. "That was... a lot."

"Your friends care about you," Devon observed. "They missed you."

Kate nodded against his shoulder. "It was strange, being back. Everything's the same, but I'm... not."

Devon understood completely. It was the fundamental challenge of his existence, remaining in a world that changed while he did not. But for Kate, the experience was reversed. She had changed, evolved, while her world had remained the same. "Is that a good thing or a bad thing?" he asked as they stepped outside onto the pavement.

Kate considered the question as they walked to their waiting car. "I don't know." She looked up at the building one last time before getting into the car. "It's just different."

***

Back in their apartment, with the city glittering below, Kate headed straight for the bathroom to wash off the lingering scent of incense and paint from the loft. Devon moved toward the kitchen to pour himself a glass of blood, but stopped short when he noticed something on the dining table that hadn't been there when they left.

A magnificent bouquet of flowers sat in an expensive crystal vase, the arrangement so elaborate and professionally done that it could only have come from the city's most exclusive florist. The blooms were unusual, deep purple mountain orchids, white alpine roses, and delicate blue gentians, all flowers that Devon recognized with a growing sense of unease.

Carpathian flowers. Flowers that grew wild in the mountains of his homeland, flowers that were nearly impossible to obtain fresh in New York unless one had very specific connections.

Devon approached the arrangement slowly, his vampire senses picking up the faint, familiar scent of the high mountain air that still clung to the petals. Nestled among the stems was a small, cream-colored card.

With careful fingers, he extracted the card and read the elegant script:

Congratulations on your beautiful exhibition. I do hope we'll have the pleasure of meeting soon.

Devon's jaw tightened as he reread the message. To anyone else, it might look like a kind congratulatory gift from someone who went to Kate's gallery opening. But Devon understood the truth. The flowers, the specific type; this was not a simple admirer. Someone from his past knew exactly where he was, knew about Kate's exhibition, and had gotten into their private apartment. Someone who wanted him to know they were watching.

"Devon?" Kate's voice called from the bathroom. "Everything okay out there?"

Devon quickly slipped the card into his jacket pocket and stepped away from the flowers. "Everything's fine," he called back, his voice carefully controlled.

When Kate emerged from the bathroom, wrapped in a robe with her hair damp around her shoulders, she immediately noticed the elaborate bouquet. "Those are gorgeous!" she exclaimed, moving toward the flowers with obvious delight. "When did these arrive? They must have cost a fortune."

Devon watched her lean in to smell the blooms, his body tense with barely controlled anxiety. "They were here when we returned. Did you order them?"

"No, but they're incredible. Look at these orchids, I've never seen anything like them." Kate examined the arrangement with an artist's eye for beauty. "There's no card?"

"No card," Devon lied smoothly. "Perhaps they're from the gallery congratulating you on the successful opening."

Kate nodded, accepting the explanation. "Miranda did mention that some collectors were very impressed. This is so thoughtful."

She continued to admire the flowers while Devon stood rigid nearby, his mind racing through possibilities and threats. Someone knew about Kate, knew about their relationship, and wanted Devon to understand that they could reach them anywhere.

Kate looked up at him, noticing his tense posture for the first time. "You seem upset. What's wrong?"

Devon forced himself to relax, moving to pour himself a drink from the bar cart they'd had delivered. "Nothing's wrong. Just tired from the evening."

But as Kate continued to fuss over the mysterious flowers, Devon's mind was already working away. The past was reaching for them with elegant, expensive fingers, and he would do whatever it took to keep Kate safe.

"I should put these in the bedroom," Kate said, lifting the heavy vase. "They're too beautiful to leave out here where we can't see them."

"Leave them here," Devon said quickly, then softened his tone when Kate looked at him in surprise. "They're quite fragrant. They might be overwhelming in the bedroom."

Kate shrugged, setting the vase back down. "You're probably right. They are pretty strong."

Later, in the early morning darkness, while Kate slept peacefully in bed, Devon stood by the window gazing at the city lights. The flowers rested on the dining table like a lovely warning, their mountain scent a continuous reminder that his past had caught up with them.

He pulled out his phone and messaged Antoine:

Need information on any unusual vampire activity in New York. Someone knows where I am.

The response came within minutes:

Will investigate. Be careful, mon ami. The old ones have long memories.

Devon deleted both messages and returned to bed, but sleep eluded him. Somewhere in the darkness of the city, someone was watching, waiting, planning. And Devon had no idea what they wanted or how far they would go to get it. All he knew was that Kate was in danger, and he would do anything to protect her. Even if it meant facing the ghosts of his past.

Chapter 7

Kate woke in complete darkness, the bedroom's blackout curtains and specialized window treatments preventing any sunlight from entering Devon's sanctuary. Beside her, he lay dormant in vampire sleep, his chest unmoving. His face was peaceful in a way that still sometimes startled her. Even after months of sharing his bed, the absolute stillness of his daylight rest unnerved her a bit.

She quietly got out of bed, using the soft light from her phone to find the bedroom door. Once she reached the hallway and closed the door behind her, she turned on the lights. She made coffee in the kitchen and stood by the window, looking out at the busy city below. Sunlight flooded the streets, contrasting sharply with the dark room she had just left.

Her phone buzzed with a text from Zoe:

Saw the Times review online. Holy shit, Kate! Lunch today? I need details.

Kate smiled, feeling a warm glow of satisfaction. The review had been everything Miranda had hoped for; it was thoughtful, appreciative, and likely to drive more visitors to the gallery.

She texted back: *Noon? That place in SoHo you love?*

Perfect. Can't wait to hear everything.

Kate spent the morning drawing in her journal and thinking about the whirlwind of the night before. At eleven-thirty, she left a note for Devon on the kitchen counter and stepped out into the bright Manhattan morning. The city felt different during the day; it felt more urgent and more human. She walked through Tribeca toward SoHo, enjoying the freedom of being just another person on the sidewalk.

Turning onto Spring Street, Kate suddenly felt an odd prickling at the back of her neck, as if someone were watching her. She looked over her left shoulder but saw nothing unusual, just the usual crowd of pedestrians.

The feeling lingered nonetheless, a subtle unease settling over her.

The restaurant Zoe had chosen was a small bistro tucked between a vintage clothing store and a bookshop, the kind of place that served excellent salads and attracted the creative crowd. Kate arrived first and claimed a table by the window, watching the stream of people pass by on the sidewalk. Zoe burst through the door ten minutes later, her wild curls barely contained by a colorful headband, paint stains on her fingers despite her obvious attempt to clean up. She spotted Kate immediately and rushed over, pulling her into a fierce hug.

"Kate Morgan, you absolute superstar!" Zoe exclaimed, loud enough to draw glances from other diners. "I cannot believe you didn't tell me about this show until yesterday!"

"It all happened so fast," Kate laughed, settling back into her chair. "Three days from phone call to opening night. I barely had time to process it myself."

Zoe flagged down a server and ordered a glass of wine despite the early hour. "Okay, I need to hear everything. Start from the beginning and don't leave out a single detail."

Kate recounted receiving Miranda's call, the hurried preparation, the installation, and the opening night itself. Zoe listened with the intense focus she brought to everything, occasionally interrupting with questions or exclamations of excitement.

"And Devon?" Zoe asked when Kate paused to take a sip of her iced tea. "How was he with all of this? I mean, it's your world, your people. That had to be weird for him."

Kate considered the question, thinking of how seamlessly Devon had navigated the gallery crowd. "He was… perfect, actually. Supportive but not overbearing. He let me have my moment while still being there for me."

"That's good," Zoe said, though Kate caught a note of something in her voice. "I was worried he might be one of those guys who gets weird about their girlfriend's success."

"He's not like that," Kate said firmly. "If anything, he's more excited about my career than I am sometimes."

Zoe studied her friend's face with the penetrating gaze that had made her such a good artist. "You look different," she said finally. "Happier. More… settled, I guess."

Kate felt warmth at the observation. "I feel different. More confident, maybe. Like I finally know who I am as an artist."

"And as a person?" The question lingered between them.

Kate thought seriously about the woman she'd been months ago compared to who she was now. "Yes," she nodded. "As a person, too."

They ordered lunch, with Kate choosing the quinoa salad she had been craving and Zoe going for the burger despite her earlier intentions to eat healthier. As they waited for their food, Zoe leaned in a little closer. "So, real talk. Are you happy? Like, genuinely happy? Because I know things started in an unusual way for you two."

Kate appreciated her friend's bluntness. Zoe had a right to be skeptical of Devon, worried about the speed with which Kate had seemingly disappeared into his world. "I am," Kate said simply. "Happier than I've ever been, actually."

Their food arrived, and they fell into the comfortable rhythm of old friends sharing a meal. Zoe updated Kate on her own work, a series of installations exploring urban decay that was gaining attention from several galleries. Kate felt a pang of guilt at how out of touch she'd been with her friend's career.

"I'm sorry I've been so absent," she said. "I know I disappeared into Devon's world pretty completely."

Zoe waved off the apology. "You were figuring things out. I get it. But I'm glad you're back in the city, at least part-time. I missed having you around."

After lunch, they walked through SoHo together, stopping in galleries and boutiques. Kate found herself seeing the old neighborhood with fresh eyes, noticing details she'd missed in her previous life as an emerging artist.

"Can I ask you something?" Zoe said as they settled on a bench near a fountain in the park.

"Of course."

"Do you ever think about the future? Like, long-term future? With Devon?"

Kate felt a familiar flutter of uncertainty. It was a question she'd been avoiding, even in her own thoughts. "What do you mean?"

"I mean, you're twenty-eight. At some point, you might want kids, a family. And he's... well, he's not exactly the settling-down-in-suburbia type."

Kate stared at the fountain, watching the water catch the afternoon light. "We haven't talked about it much," she admitted. "We're still figuring everything out."

"So you do think about it?"

"Sometimes." Kate turned to face her friend. "The thing is, Zoe, what we have is so intense, so consuming, that sometimes the future feels irrelevant. Like we're living in this perfect bubble where normal concerns don't apply."

Zoe's expression grew concerned. "But bubbles burst, Kate. And when they do, then what?"

The words hit hard because they raised fears Kate had been ignoring. What would her future with Devon be like? What did a long-term relationship with a centuries-old vampire really involve?

"I know you're worried about me," Kate said softly. "And I appreciate it. But I need you to trust that I know what I'm doing."

"Do you, though?" Zoe's voice was gentle but persistent. "Because from the outside, it looks like you've completely reorganized your life around someone else's schedule, someone else's needs."

Kate felt a flash of irritation. "That's not fair. Devon has been incredibly supportive of my art."

"I'm not saying he's not supportive. I'm saying that support and partnership aren't the same thing. Can you honestly tell me that you have equal say in the major decisions in your relationship?"

The question hit harder than Kate expected. She thought about their living arrangements, their travel plans, even their daily routines, how much of it was shaped by Devon's needs as a vampire versus her needs as a human?

"It's complicated," she said finally.

"It doesn't have to be," Zoe replied. "Look, I like Devon. He seems to genuinely care about you, and he's obviously good for your art. But I need to know that you're not losing yourself in this relationship."

Kate sat in silence for a moment, watching a group of NYU students play frisbee on the grass. "I'm not losing myself," she said eventually. "I'm becoming myself. The person I was before Devon… she was scared, slow to trust, playing it safe. This version of me is braver, more confident, more willing to take risks."

"And that's great," Zoe said. "But make sure that brave, confident woman is making choices for herself, not just following someone else's lead."

They sat in comfortable silence after that, each lost in their own thoughts. Kate appreciated Zoe's concern, even if it made her uncomfortable. Her friend was asking questions Kate had been avoiding, forcing her to examine aspects of her relationship she'd been content to leave unquestioned.

As the afternoon wore on, they made their way back toward Tribeca. Kate felt a familiar pull as the sun began to sink below the skyline, knowing that Devon would soon wake, and their evening together was approaching. It was a feeling she'd grown to love, the anticipation of reconnecting after the solitude of the day.

"I should head home," she said as they reached the corner where their paths would diverge.

"Of course you should," Zoe said with a knowing smile. "Your mysterious European is probably wondering where you are."

"He's not mysterious," Kate protested, laughing despite herself.

"Right. Just wealthy, reclusive, and keeps unusual hours." Zoe hugged her tightly. "I'm happy for you, Kate. Really. I just want to make sure you stay happy."

"I will," Kate promised. "And I'll be better about staying in touch. Maybe we can make this a regular thing, the lunch dates."

"I'd like that," Zoe said. "And Kate? Congratulations again on the show.

You deserve it."

Kate walked the last few blocks to her building, thinking about her day. The lunch with Zoe had been just what she needed. It connected her to her human side and reminded her of who she had been before Devon. It also gently pushed her to think about who she was becoming.

The feeling of being watched had faded while they were in Washington Square Park. But now, as she walked alone through the quieter streets of Tribeca, it came back. Kate found herself glancing at shop windows, using the reflections to check behind her. She didn't see anything unusual, just the usual late-afternoon foot traffic of people heading home or running errands. Still, she walked a bit faster, wanting to reach the safety of her building.

Zoe's questions stayed on her mind. Was she losing herself in their relationship? Was she just following Devon's lead? These questions made her uneasy because they touched on truths she wasn't ready to confront.

She opened the apartment door to find Devon in the kitchen, his hair still tousled from sleep, pouring himself a glass of blood. He looked up as she entered, his face lighting up with a smile that made her heart skip.

"How was your day?" he asked, crossing to kiss her softly.

"Perfect," Kate said, and realized she meant it. "How was your sleep?"

"Restful. I dreamed of you at the gallery, radiant and confident." He studied her face with the intensity that never failed to make her feel seen. "You look thoughtful. Good day with Zoe?"

Kate nodded, settling onto one of the barstools. "She's worried about me. About us."

Devon's expression grew serious. "What kind of worried?"

"The usual best friend concerns. Whether I'm happy, whether I'm making my own choices, whether I'm thinking about the future."

Devon was quiet for a moment, processing her words. "And what did you tell her?"

"That I'm happier than I've ever been. That I trust us to figure out the future as we go." Kate paused, studying his face. "But her questions made me think. We don't really talk about the long term much, do we?"

"No," Devon admitted. "I suppose I've been afraid to presume too much about what you want."

"And I've been afraid to ask for too much," Kate said softly. They looked at each other across the kitchen island. Unsaid possibilities hung between them and Kate felt the same flutter of uncertainty she had felt in the park. But she also sensed a stronger feeling of rightness. She wanted a future with Devon, no matter what challenges lay ahead. "Maybe it's time we started talking about it," she said.

Devon's smile was gentle and full of promise. "I would like that." Watching the moon rise over Manhattan, Kate felt whole. She had spent time with her best friend, reflected on her choices, and reconnected with her independent self. But now, as evening approached and Devon fully awoke, she was ready to return to their shared world.

The questions Zoe had raised weren't going away, and Kate knew they would need to face them eventually. But for now, it was enough to know that she was choosing this life, this love, this partnership with full awareness of what it meant.

She was no longer the uncertain woman she had been when she first met Devon. She was an artist with a successful gallery showing, a woman with deep friendships and professional recognition, someone who could spend a day exploring the city on her own and return home confident in her choices.

The daylight hours had reminded her of who she was outside of her relationship with Devon. And rather than that knowledge creating distance between them, it made her more certain than ever that she wanted to build a future with him. Not as Devon's captive or his Pet, but as his equal and his partner. The woman she had become was strong enough for whatever came next.

Chapter 8

It had been a mentally heavier day than Kate had originally expected. She retreated to the bathroom, turning on the shower and letting steam fill the marble space. Hot water fell over her shoulders, easing muscles still pleasantly sore from recent intimacies with Devon. Lost in thought, she didn't hear the bathroom door open. The glass shower door creaked, and suddenly Devon was behind her, his cool skin a stark contrast to the steaming water.

"Room for one more?" he murmured, his hands sliding around her waist. Kate leaned back against him, feeling the solid planes of his chest against her back. "Always."

Devon reached for a bottle of shampoo, pouring a small pool into his palm. He worked it gently through her hair, his fingers massaging her scalp with an exquisite, practiced pressure that drew a soft sigh from her lips. He moved with a slow, deliberate tenderness, his focus entirely on the task, her. He rinsed her hair until it was squeaking clean, his hands careful and sure.

"I could get used to this," Kate sighed, eyes closed in bliss.

"I've never washed another person's hair before," Devon mused out loud. "It's strangely intimate."

Kate turned to face him, the water sluicing between them. "More intimate than what we did last night?"

He smiled. "It's a different kind of intimate. That was passion. This is… care."

Kate's heart melted at his words. She took the bar of soap, working it into a rich lather between her hands. "Then let me care for you, too."

She ran her slick hands over his chest, his shoulders, his arms, her touch lingering. It wasn't a prelude to sex, but something else entirely. It was an act of mapping, learning, devotion. She was tending to him, caring for the body of this ancient, powerful creature who had, against all odds, given her his heart. It was a tender ritual that felt more profound than any passionate encounter.

As he worked the soap over her body, Devon leaned down to graze his teeth along the curve of her neck in affection and adoration. But this time, instead of the usual playful shiver, Kate felt a deeper longing.

"Don't stop," she whispered, tilting her head to give him better access.

"Okay," Devon whispered against her skin, his fangs lengthening as he moved to touch the smooth curve where her neck met her shoulder. Kate gasped softly at the sharp feeling of his fangs breaking her skin, quickly followed by a wave of pleasure that made her lean more against him. Devon groaned low in his throat as the taste of her and the intimacy of the moment overwhelmed his senses.

Kate watched, captivated, as thin streams of blood ran down her collarbone and over the curve of her breast. The red liquid mixed with the warm shower water as it flowed over her body. The scene was oddly beautiful, intimate, and primal in a moment that felt like theirs alone.

When Devon finally withdrew, he pressed tender kisses to the small wounds, his tongue soothing the marks he'd left. Kate turned in his arms, feeling bonded to him in a way that went beyond words.

When they finally emerged from the shower, pink-skinned and wrapped in plush towels, Kate felt a sense of connection that was transcendental.

"I have a surprise for you," she said as she combed through her wet hair. "There's a collection of historical instruments at the Met. They have a private viewing tonight for patrons. I called and pulled some strings," she said, a hint of pride in her voice. "I thought you could show me a piece of your world. The one before."

"You planned this?" Devon's expression softened in astonishment.

Kate nodded shyly. "I want to show you that I'm trying to understand your world too."

Devon held her close. "Thank you," he whispered into her wet hair. "It's a wonderful surprise."

* * *

An elderly curator guided them through the halls of the Metropolitan Museum of Art to the wing with the instrument collection. Devon moved from one display to the next, centuries of musical history resting behind glass, excitement shining in his eyes.

"I studied with a man who played one of these," he said as he pointed to a 17th-century viola da gamba with dark, rich wood. His fingers moved of their own accord with nostalgia, tracing patterns in the air as though playing invisible strings.

Kate watched, transfixed, as his hands performed a dance they had learned centuries ago. He led her to a display of early keyboard instruments, stopping before a virginal from the 1600s. "My mother played one of these," he said softly.

Kate watched him, her heart aching. This was the boy from before the vampire "Tell me more about her," she encouraged gently.

Devon's gaze grew distant. "She was... kind. Gentle. She taught me everything. My father thought music was a frivolous pursuit, but she insisted that beauty had value of its own."

His hand drifted to his throat, fingers absently tracing what appeared to be a thin, silvery scar at the base of his neck. So faded it was nearly invisible, yet his fingers found it unerringly, as if drawn by muscle memory centuries old.

"She sounds wonderful," Kate said softly.

"She was." Devon's voice held centuries of loss. "She died when I was young. Childbirth. The baby, a girl, died too."

Kate reached out, her hand finding his. He turned his hand to clasp hers, his touch cool, but comforting.

"What happened to him?" Kate asked, finally. "The boy you were."

Devon's eyes met hers, centuries of memory in their depths. For a moment, he seemed to look through her, beyond her, to another time. His body went rigid, his pupils dilating slightly. A flash of memory seemed to pass across his face, candlelight reflecting on dark wood paneling, the sound of a harpsichord echoing through a grand salon, a woman's pale hand adorned with rubies extending toward him…

"He died in Vienna in 1623," Devon said, his voice suddenly hoarse. "Officially, of a fever."

Devon's hand moved to his throat again, this time more deliberately, revealing the silvery scar Kate had glimpsed earlier. "In reality, at the hands of a beautiful noblewoman who had taken an interest in his musical compositions."

"Elisabeta, your maker?" Kate said, the name falling between them like a stone.

Devon recoiled at the sound of the name, a reaction so visceral and immediate that Kate knew it wasn't voluntary. His eyes darted to the darkened doorway of the gallery, as if expecting someone to materialize there.

"Yes," he whispered, his voice dropping so low Kate had to lean closer. "She kept me for fifty years."

He closed his eyes briefly, and when he opened them, Kate saw something she'd never witnessed before, a momentary flash of crimson in his irises, quickly suppressed.

"She taught me what it meant to be vampire," he said, his voice flat, controlled with visible effort. "To hunt. To kill."

His hand trembled slightly as he reached out to touch the glass protecting the virginal, as if seeking an anchor to the present. Kate noticed his reflection in the glass, distorted, wavering, somehow less substantial than it should be.

"The worst part wasn't the killing," he continued, his voice dropping further. "It was the bond."

He turned to Kate, his expression haunted. "Imagine feeling someone's thoughts inside your mind. Their desires become your desires. Their anger becomes your rage. Their will…" He trailed off, shuddering. "She could pull me to her from across the city," he said. "I would feel it here—" he touched his sternum, "—like a hook behind my ribs, dragging me back to her no matter how far I ran."

Kate felt a chill, understanding now the true nature of the maker bond he had hinted at before. Devon suddenly stiffened, his head turning sharply toward the museum entrance, nostrils flaring slightly. For a moment, he seemed to be listening to something Kate couldn't hear, his entire body alert like a predator sensing danger.

"Devon?" Kate asked, alarmed by the sudden change.

He seemed to force himself to relax with visible effort. His eyes kept darting around the shadows. "It's nothing, just… memories. When I finally escaped during the fire that killed her," he continued after a pause, his voice low, "I promised I would never let anyone control me again. I spent centuries building walls around my mind."

As he spoke, Kate noticed his pupils contract to pinpoints, then dilate again, a subtle but inhuman reaction that reminded her of his true nature.

"And then you met me," Kate said quietly, understanding the terrible parallel.

Devon's expression softened, the unnatural tension in his body easing. "And then I met you. And learned that there are different kinds of control. Different kinds of captivity."

"We've both come a long way," she said, her voice thick with emotion.

Devon lifted her hand to his lips, pressing a kiss to her palm.

"We have," he said softly.

As they moved to leave the gallery, Devon paused once more, his head turning sharply toward a darkened corridor. This time, Kate was certain she saw fear flash across his face, ancient, primal fear that had nothing to do with the man he was now and everything to do with the boy he had been in Vienna, centuries ago.

"Devon?" she asked again. "What is it?"

He shook his head, taking her arm with gentle firmness. "Nothing," he said, but his eyes remained fixed on the shadows. "Let's go home."

Kate allowed him to guide her toward the exit, but she couldn't shake the feeling that something had changed, that in speaking of Elisabeta, they had somehow summoned more than just memories.

Chapter 9

Kate had never dined in a restaurant like this before she met Devon. Nestled in a quiet townhouse in the Upper East Side, it had no sign, no website, and no social media presence. The only way to dine there was through a personal invitation from the owner —or, in their case, through Devon's seemingly limitless connections and resources.

Their private dining area was a study in understated luxury. Walls paneled in dark wood, a single table set with gleaming silver and crystal, and lighting so perfectly positioned that Kate felt as though she were glowing from within. A fire crackled in a small hearth, casting dancing shadows across the room.

"This is ridiculous," Kate said, but she was smiling as she took another bite of her truffle risotto. "I'm pretty sure this meal costs more than my monthly rent." Devon watched her eat with evident pleasure, his own plate arranged to give the impression he'd been enjoying his food. "Worth every penny to see you enjoy it," he said. "Besides, the chef is an old friend."

"Let me guess, you saved his great-grandfather from bankruptcy during the Great Depression?"

Devon's lips twitched. "His grandmother, actually. Vienna, 1952."

Kate shook her head, still adjusting to the casual way Devon referenced history he'd personally witnessed. "Of course. Silly me." The sommelier appeared with a fresh glass of wine for Kate, bowing slightly before retreating. Devon had arranged everything in advance, a seven-course tasting menu for Kate, paired with wines from vineyards she'd never heard of, and discreet service that materialized and vanished with minimal intrusion.

Devon's phone vibrated on the table. He glanced at it casually, then froze, his expression shifting so quickly that Kate might have missed it if she hadn't been watching him closely. "Everything okay?" she asked.

Devon's face smoothed into a neutral mask as he slipped the phone into his pocket. "Just business. Nothing that can't wait until tomorrow night."

But Kate had seen the flash of something in his eyes—alarm? Fear? Whatever it was, it vanished behind his practiced composure. "Devon," she said, setting down her fork. "What is it?"

"Nothing to concern yourself with," he said, signaling for the check. "Are you finished? We should get back to the apartment. It's getting late."

Kate frowned. Devon never rushed their evenings together, typically lingering over conversation until the early hours of the morning. Something had changed in the last thirty seconds. "I was actually thinking about dessert," she said, testing him.

"We will have to take a rain check on dessert," Devon replied, already standing. "I've suddenly remembered an important call I need to make." As the waiter appeared with the check, Kate watched Devon's eyes scan the restaurant's main dining room through their partially open door. His posture had changed, too; he was more alert. She'd seen this side of him before, but rarely since they'd become true partners.

Something was very wrong.

In the car, Devon sat closer to Kate than usual, one arm draped possessively around her shoulders. His other hand held his phone, thumb scrolling through messages too quickly for her to read. Every few blocks, his eyes would flick to the rearview mirror, tracking the traffic behind them.

"What's going on, Devon?" Kate finally asked, her patience running out.

"It's complicated," Devon said, still distracted.

"I'm pretty quick; I think I can keep up," Kate said dryly.

Devon's lips pressed into a thin line. "It's vampire business."

"Right." Kate moved slightly away from him. "And I'm just the fragile human who couldn't possibly understand."

Devon sighed, tucking his phone away and turning to face her fully. "That's not what I meant."

"Then what did you mean?"

Before Devon could answer, the car pulled up to their apartment building. "We'll discuss it upstairs," he said, his tone making it clear the conversation was temporarily on pause. The doorman in the lobby nodded respectfully as Devon guided Kate toward the private elevator with a hand at the small of her back. "Mr Karlov," the doorman called, stepping forward. "A package was delivered for you earlier. It was sent up to your apartment."

Devon tensed beside her. "When exactly was it delivered? And by whom?" The doorman consulted his log. "At 10:30 PM, sir. A courier service. Standard protocol was followed; it was scanned and cleared by security."

Devon seemed to consider this for a moment, then gave a tight nod. In the elevator, Kate crossed her arms. "A package at this hour? More 'vampire business'?"

Devon's jaw tightened. "Kate, please. I promise I'll explain everything once we're inside."

The elevator opened right into their penthouse apartment. Devon stepped out first and looked around the space before letting Kate enter. This level of protection might have seemed sweet at another time, but now it only increased her worry. A small, simply wrapped box rested on a sleek console table by the door.

He moved through the apartment methodically, checking rooms, closing curtains that were already closed, and testing the locks on doors and windows. Kate watched from the center of the living room, her worry giving way to irritation.

"Devon, you're scaring me," she said finally. "Either tell me what's happening or stop acting like we're about to be attacked." Devon paused, his back to her as he gazed out at the New York skyline through a narrow gap in the curtains. For a long moment, he said nothing. Then, with a deep breath, he turned to face her. "I received a warning," he said, his voice carefully controlled. "From Antoine."

"What kind of warning?"

Devon crossed to the bar and poured himself a glass of blood from a crystal decanter, his own private stock. He took a long drink before answering.

"Here," he said, pulling out his phone and handing it to her. "See for yourself."

The message was brief:

> *She has been watching. She knows about Kate. Take precautions. Will call with details.*

Kate read it twice, a chill creeping up her spine despite the warmth of the apartment. "She? Who is 'she'?"

Devon took another drink, emptying the glass. "Someone from my past. Someone dangerous."

"That's not an answer, Devon." Kate set the phone down on the coffee table between them. "You've been acting like we're being hunted since you got this message. I deserve to know why."

Devon refilled his glass, a sign of stress that Kate had learned to recognize. "It's complicated," he said again.

"Stop saying that." Kate's voice rose slightly. "We're supposed to be partners now. That means you don't get to decide what I'm allowed to know about threats to our safety."

Devon's eyes flashed with something, frustration, perhaps, or fear. "You're right," he said after a moment. "You deserve to know. But it's... difficult for me to explain."

Kate softened slightly. "Then just start at the beginning. Who is she?"

Devon sank onto the sofa, suddenly looking weary in a way vampires rarely did. "Someone who once had power over me. Someone I thought, hoped, was out of my life forever."

Kate sat beside him, leaving space between them. "An ex-lover?"

A bitter laugh erupted from his throat, incredulous to him. "Lover implies a mutual consent that was... lacking." The implication hung in the air between them. Kate felt a surge of protectiveness Devon, even as her frustration at his evasiveness remained.

"Devon," she said gently, "just tell me. Whatever it is, we'll face it together."

He looked at her then, his ancient eyes filled with a vulnerability that made her heart ache. "I need to make some calls first. Talk to Antoine to ensure your safety."

"My safety?"

"If she knows about you—" Devon broke off, his hand tightening around the crystal glass until Kate feared it might shatter. "I won't let her near you. I promise you that."

"Devon—"

He held up a hand, his attention fixed on the package on the console table. "Stay here."

Kate remained on the sofa, watching as he approached the box. He examined it without touching it. "Aren't you going to open it?" she asked.

"Not yet." Devon took out his phone. "I need to make that call first. Will you excuse me for a moment?"

Kate nodded, mustering all her will to wait for him. Devon stepped onto the terrace, closing the glass door behind him. Through the curtains, Kate could see his silhouette, phone pressed to his ear, pacing back and forth in the night air.

She looked at the package on the table. It was small, perhaps six inches square, wrapped in plain brown paper with no markings except for Devon's name and their address written in elegant handwriting. No return address.

Devon's voice rose on the terrace, the words indistinct but the tone unmistakably urgent. Kate had never heard him sound so agitated, so afraid. Kate's gaze returned to the package. Whatever was happening, the answers were likely inside that box. Devon would be angry if she opened it, but he was already keeping secrets from her. Partners didn't do that. Decision made, she reached for the package.

The paper came away easily, revealing a black velvet box underneath. Kate hesitated, then lifted the lid. Inside, nestled on black satin, was a small silver hand mirror, antique by the look of it. Kate lifted it carefully, turning it over in her hands. The back was engraved with an intricate design of flowers and vines surrounding what appeared to be a family crest.

It seemed harmless enough, if oddly personal. Why would this cause such alarm? She turned the mirror over to examine her reflection and gasped. In the glass, she saw not only herself but also a woman standing behind her, a woman who was not in the room. Pale and beautiful, with dark hair cascading over bare shoulders and eyes that seemed to burn with an inner light. The woman smiled, revealing the delicate points of vampire fangs, and raised a finger to her lips in a gesture of silence.

Kate dropped the mirror, a scream caught in her throat. It landed on the plush carpet with a soft thud, face down. The terrace door slid open, and Devon was beside her in an instant. "What happened? Are you hurt?" His hands moved over her, checking for injuries.

"The mirror," Kate managed, pointing to where it lay on the floor. "There was a woman—"

Devon followed her gaze, his body going stiff when he saw the open box and the mirror beside it. "You opened it," he said, his voice flat.

"Yes, I—"

"What did you see?" Devon demanded, gripping her shoulders. "Kate, this is important. What exactly did you see?"

"A woman," Kate said, her voice shaking slightly. "Behind me in the reflection. Beautiful, dark-haired. She smiled at me, I saw fangs. And then she put her finger to her lips, like she was telling me to keep a secret."

Devon released her and stepped back, his expression shifting from concern to something closer to dread. "Elisabeta," he whispered.

Kate felt a cold weight settle in her stomach. "Your maker? But you told me she was killed centuries ago. That she died in a fire?"

"I lied." The words hung between them, heavy with implication.

"You lied," Kate repeated slowly. "About something that important."

Devon set the package aside and reached for her hands, but Kate pulled away. "Why?" she asked. "Why would you lie about that?"

"Because I was ashamed," Devon said, his voice low. "Because I didn't want you to know the truth about my creation. About what I was to her."

"And what was that?"

Devon's eyes met hers, centuries of pain visible in their depths. "Her Pet," he said simply. "Her possession. Her toy." The word 'Pet' landed between them like a stone, heavy with the history of their own relationship's beginning. Kate felt sick.

"She's still alive? All this time? And you never thought to mention that?" Kate stood, needing distance between them. "All those conversations we had about your past, about vampire society, about your life before me, and you never once thought to mention that your maker is still out there?"

Devon's face was a mask of regret. "I wanted to forget her. To pretend she didn't exist. And for long stretches of time, I could. Years would pass without sighting her."

"But she's been watching you all this time?" Kate said, remembering the message.

"Periodically," Devon admitted. "She… checks in. Reminds me that she knows where I am, what I'm doing. It's a game to her."

"A game," Kate echoed hollowly.

"She's never interfered directly in my life. Not since I left her. She just observes. Sends little reminders of her existence."

"Like the mirror."

"Yes."

Kate wrapped her arms around herself, suddenly cold despite the warmth of the suite. "And now she knows about me."

Devon stood, moving toward her, but stopped when Kate took a step back. "Yes," he said again. "And that changes everything."

Kate thought of the woman in the mirror, her beautiful, terrible smile. "She was warning me," she realized. "Showing me she can reach me, even when you're right outside the door."

Devon's expression darkened. "Yes."

"What does she want?" Kate asked again.

"I don't know," Devon repeated. "But I intend to find out."

Kate turned away from him and moved to the window to look out at the city lights. Her mind raced as she tried to make sense of this new information and everything she thought she knew about Devon.

"You should have told me," she finally said. "From the beginning."

"I know," Devon replied. His voice was closer now, but he still kept a respectful distance. "I was wrong to keep it from you. I thought I was protecting you."

"No," Kate said, turning to face him. "You were protecting yourself. From having to talk about it. From having to remember."

Devon didn't deny it. "Yes," he said simply. "That too."

Kate felt tears threatening and blinked them back. She wouldn't cry, not now. "What happens next?"

"I need to speak with Antoine again. Get more information. Then we'll decide what comes next."

"We?" Kate raised an eyebrow. "Suddenly, I'm included in the decision-making?"

Devon flinched slightly at her tone. "Kate, please. I know I've handled this badly. But we're in danger, you're in danger, and I need you to trust me."

"Trust works both ways, Devon." Kate moved past him, heading for the bedroom. "Make your calls. Get your information. But when you're done, I expect the whole truth. No more convenient omissions."

She closed the bedroom door behind her, leaning against it as the tears she'd been holding back finally spilled over. Through the door, she could hear Devon speaking in rapid Hungarian, his voice tense and urgent.

Kate moved to the bed and sat on the edge, trying to process everything she'd learned. Devon had lied to her, not just once, but consistently, over months of intimate conversations about his past. His maker was alive. And now this ancient vampire had taken an interest in her.

She lay down on the bed, still fully dressed, and stared at the ceiling. Sleep seemed impossible, but she closed her eyes anyway, hoping for a brief respite from the turmoil of her thoughts. Instead, she dreamed.

Kate was walking through a grand ballroom, empty except for herself and the echoing sound of her footsteps. Overhead chandeliers sparkled, their crystals catching the light. At the far end of the ballroom stood a woman in a red gown, her back to Kate. Dark hair cascaded down her pale shoulders, just as it had in the mirror. Kate knew she should turn and run, but her feet carried her forward instead, drawn by a curiosity she couldn't suppress.

"Hello, Kate Morgan," the woman said without turning. Her voice was melodic, with an accent Kate couldn't quite place, older than Devon's, with different

inflections.

"Elisabeta," Kate replied, the name falling from her lips like she'd spoken it a thousand times before.

The woman turned, and Kate saw her face clearly for the first time. She was beautiful, beyond conventional standards, with perfectly symmetrical features. Her skin was radiant, and her eyes a deep, burning amber that seemed to glow. The woman smiled, her red lips forming a smile that revealed the delicate tips of fangs. "He was mine first, you know, for longer than your entire family has existed."

"He doesn't belong to anyone," Kate heard herself say. "Not anymore."

Elisabeta laughed, the sound like crystal bells. "Oh, sweet girl. You understand so little." She moved closer, her movements fluid and predatory. Kate wanted to step back, but found herself frozen in place.

"What do you want?" Kate asked, echoing her question from the waking world.

Elisabeta reached out, her cool fingers tracing the line of Kate's jaw. "To see what has captured my creation's heart so completely. To understand what makes you special."

"I'm not special," Kate said. "I'm just human."

"No," Elisabeta murmured, leaning in until her lips nearly brushed Kate's ear. "There's something more. Something he sees in you. I intend to discover what that is."

She pulled back slightly, her amber eyes boring into Kate's. "He was mine first," she repeated, this time in Hungarian. "And what was mine always returns to me in the end."

Kate woke with a gasp, sitting bolt upright in the bed. The room was dark except for a thin line of light under the door. Her heart pounded in her chest, the dream still vivid in her mind. The bedroom door opened, and Devon stood silhouetted in the doorway. "Kate?" he said softly. "Are you alright? I heard you cry out."

Kate pressed a hand to her chest, willing her heart to slow. "I had a dream," she said. "About her."

Devon was beside her in an instant, the mattress dipping under his weight. "Tell me," he said, his voice urgent.

Kate described the dream, the ballroom, Elisabeta's appearance, and their conversation. With each detail, Devon's expression grew more troubled. "She spoke to me in Hungarian," Kate finished. "She said, 'He was mine first. And what was mine always returns to me in the end.'"

Devon stood up quickly and moved to the window. The first light of dawn was brightening the eastern sky. "It wasn't just a dream," he said, facing away from her. "It was contact."

"Contact?" Kate asked again. "You mean she was really in my mind?"

"Yes." Devon turned to look at her, his face serious. "The mirror was a way for her to connect with you."

"Is she… still there? In my head?"

"No. The connection is temporary, especially with humans. But she can reestablish it now that it's been made once."

Kate felt violated, exposed in a way that went beyond physical vulnerability. "How do we stop her?"

"There are ways," Devon said. "But first, I need to tell you everything. No more secrets." He moved back to the bed, sitting beside her but not touching her. "The sun will be up soon," he said. "I don't have much time before sleep takes me. But I'll tell you what I can."

Kate nodded, drawing her knees up to her chest. "I'm listening."

Devon took a deep breath that he didn't need, a human gesture he'd adopted over centuries of mimicry. "I was born in 1600, in a small village outside Budapest. My father was a minor noble, my mother died when I was young. I was the second son, with no inheritance to speak of, so I was sent to Vienna to study music when I showed some talent for it."

Kate had heard parts of this story before, but she remained silent, letting him continue.

"I was thirty-two when I met Elisabeta. She presented herself as a wealthy widow with an interest in the arts. She attended every one of my performances, commissioned pieces from me, and invited me to private concerts at her estate." Devon's voice took on a distant quality, as if he were seeing it all again. "I was flattered by her attention. Seduced by it. I had no idea what she was until the night she turned me."

"Did you choose it?" Kate asked softly. "The turning?"

Devon's laugh was hollow. "No. She drugged my wine, fed from me until I was near death, then forced her blood down my throat. I awoke three days later in a locked chamber in her estate, ravenous and confused."

Kate reached for his hand then, her anger temporarily set aside in the face of his pain. Devon squeezed her fingers gratefully.

"What followed was… education, she called it. Training. She taught me to feed, to hunt, to kill. And when I resisted, when my humanity rebelled against taking innocent lives, she punished me. Starved me. Locked me away in darkness until my hunger overcame my conscience."

"Devon," Kate whispered, horrified.

"She kept me isolated from other vampires, from any contact that wasn't controlled by her. I was her creation, her possession." He spat the last word with a bitterness Kate had never heard from him before.

"How did you escape?"

"Patience. Planning. And a fire that destroyed half her estate and provided enough chaos for me to flee." Devon's eyes met hers. "I told you once that I understood what it was to put your trust in someone's hands and have it broken. Now you know why."

Kate felt a chill at the parallel between his experience and her own early days at Devon's estate. "Is that why you took me? Because it was done to you?"

Devon flinched. "No. God, no. I never made that connection until… until you helped me see what I was doing." He looked away. "I've spent centuries trying not to become her. I thought I'd succeeded."

"You're nothing like her," Kate said firmly, surprising herself with the certainty in her voice despite her lingering anger. "You recognized your mistakes and changed."

"Did I?" Devon's voice was barely audible. "Or did I just find a more subtle form of control?" Before Kate could respond, Devon continued. "After I escaped, I spent decades looking over my shoulder. I practiced strengthening my mental shields to protect myself against her will and compulsions. I expected her to hunt me down, but she never did. Instead, she would appear randomly throughout the centuries. at a distance, watching. Sometimes decades or even a century would pass without a sign of her. Then she would send a gift, a message, a reminder that she knew exactly where I was."

"Why? What does she want?"

"Control," Devon said simply. "The knowledge that she can still affect me, still make me fear her, even from a distance. It's a game to her, as I said. A very long game."

"And now she's targeting me," Kate said. "Why? Jealousy?"

"It's more than that. Elisabeta doesn't form attachments the way humans do, or even the way most vampires do. To her, I'm still her creation, her property. And you…" He hesitated.

"What about me?"

"You've done what she never could," Devon said softly. "You've claimed my heart. My true loyalty. She must find that… intriguing. Threatening, perhaps."

Kate absorbed this, trying to understand the mind of a being so ancient and alien. "What will she do?"

"I don't know," Devon said. "That's what terrifies me. In all the centuries I've known her, I've never been able to predict her actions."

Outside, the sky was lightening, the first direct rays of sunlight not far off. Devon's movements were becoming slower, his speech slightly slurred, signs of the approaching vampire sleep that would claim him with the dawn.

"We should leave New York," he said, fighting against the lethargy creeping through his system. "As soon as the sun sets tonight. Go back to the estate where I can better protect you."

"No," Kate said firmly. "I won't run. And I won't let her drive me away from my family, my friends, my work."

"Kate, please. You don't understand how dangerous she is."

"Then help me understand. When you wake tonight, tell me everything, every interaction you've had with her over the centuries, every pattern you've observed. If we're going to face her, I need to know what we're dealing with."

Devon's eyes were growing heavy, his body preparing for the deathlike sleep of daylight hours.

"Promise me you won't leave the suite today," he managed to say. "Not for anything. Keep the curtains closed. Don't let anyone in."

"I promise," Kate said, helping him lie back on the bed as his limbs grew heavier.

"The package," Devon murmured, his voice fading. "Put it in the safe. Don't touch the mirror again."

"I won't," Kate assured him, pulling the covers over his increasingly still form.

"Kate," Devon whispered, fighting against the encroaching sleep for one last moment of consciousness. "I'm sorry. For lying. For putting you in danger."

Kate brushed his hair back from his forehead, her touch gentle despite her lingering hurt.

"We'll talk about it tonight," she said. "Just rest now."

Devon's eyes closed, his body going completely still in the unnatural stillness of vampire sleep. Kate sat beside him for a long moment, watching his face, peaceful now, free from the tension and fear that had marked it throughout the night.

Finally, she rose and moved to the living room. The package still sat on the coffee table, innocuous-looking in its plain brown wrapper. Kate picked it up carefully, carried it to the safe in the closet, and locked it away as Devon had instructed. Then she drew the blackout curtains tighter, checking that no stray beam of sunlight could reach Devon's sleeping form, and settled into an armchair to wait for nightfall.

Outside, New York awakened to a new day, unaware of the ancient vampire who had just announced her presence in their midst. Kate watched the thin line of sunlight at the edge of the curtains and thought of the woman from her dream, beautiful, terrible, and fixated on the man Kate loved.

"What was mine always returns to me in the end," Elisabeta had said.

"We'll see about that," Kate whispered to the empty room.

Chapter 10

Kate watched the city, alive and thrumming with energy, from the living room window. She watched people move along sidewalks, listened to the sounds of taxis honking. Usually, she would sketch, catch up on emails, or simply enjoy the quiet during these hours she had to herself. But today was upheaved by the overwhelming weight of Devon's confession.

I lied.

She kept repeating the words in her mind. He hadn't just left out the truth; he had created a fantasy, a comforting tale about a dead maker. This story had allowed Kate to feel safe and to build her trust in him on a base of lies. She stepped away from the window and sat at the desk, opening her sketchbook. Her pencil started to draw the features of the woman from her dream, Elisabeta. High cheekbones, full lips curved in that knowing smile, eyes that seemed to burn even in graphite.

Drawing had always helped Kate clear her head and translate her emotions into visuals when words failed her. Now, as Elisabeta's face emerged on the page, Kate tried to make sense of her tangled feelings. Her pencil moved faster, harder, the lines becoming darker as her anger built.

She understood fear and shame—Fuck knows she had her own demons— but this was a deliberate deception about something incredibly significant. After everything they'd been through, after all the progress they'd made toward a relationship built on trust, he'd kept this from her.

She tried to remember moments when Devon could have, should have, told her the truth. The nights spent talking about his past, about the centuries he'd witnessed. Each memory was now tainted, and each shared vulnerability felt like a calculated manipulation.

Kate kept adding details to her sketch, the period-appropriate dress from her dream, the delicate fangs partially visible behind those smiling lips, the ancient intelligence in those eyes. The woman who had shaped Devon, who had held him captive, who had taught him what it meant to possess another being. The irony wasn't lost on Kate. Devon had done to her what Elisabeta had done to him, taken her captive, controlled her environment.

Though Devon had recognized his wrong and had changed, giving Kate back her agency. He had worked to become her partner rather than her captor. Or had he? The insidious thought crept in unwelcome. If he was still keeping secrets this big, still picking and choosing what she should know, was their relationship really as equal as she'd believed?

Kate closed the sketchbook with more force than necessary. She needed to move, to breathe. The suite suddenly felt too small, too confined, too much like the beautiful prison Devon's estate had once been. But she'd promised not to leave. Even though she was angry, she wouldn't break that promise, not with Elisabeta potentially watching, waiting for her to let her guard down.

Instead, Kate made lunch, took a long shower, and tried to distract herself with television. Nothing helped. Her mind kept circling back to the same questions, the same hurt, the same fear that perhaps she'd been fooling herself all along about how much Devon had really changed.

As the afternoon wore on, Kate found herself watching the clock, both dreading and anticipating sunset. They needed to talk, really talk, but she wasn't sure she was ready to hear what Devon might say.

* * *

Devon awoke with Kate's name on his lips, his body tensing before his eyes even opened. He'd spent the daylight hours in the strange half-consciousness of vampire sleep, not dreaming exactly, but aware on some level of Kate's presence in the apartment, of her movements, her emotions.

He found her sitting in an armchair across the room, watching him. Her posture was rigid, her expression guarded in a way he hadn't seen since their earliest days together. "Kate," he said softly, sitting up. "You stayed."

"I said I would." Her voice was neutral, giving nothing away.

Devon rose, moving with deliberate slowness, as if afraid any sudden movement might startle her. "Thank you."

Kate didn't respond, just continued to watch him with those steady eyes that seemed to see through all his carefully constructed facades.

"You're still angry," he observed, stopping a few feet from her chair.

"I'm not angry, Devon. I'm hurt. There's a difference."

Devon nodded, accepting the correction. "Can I sit?" he asked, gesturing to the sofa near her chair.

Kate nodded once, and Devon settled onto the edge of the sofa, his posture as tense as hers.

"I owe you more of an explanation," he began.

"Yes, you do. You deliberately lied to me, Devon," Kate whispered.

"I know," Devon said quietly. "And I'm sorry. More sorry than I can express."

"Why?" Kate demanded. "Why lie about this specific thing?"

Devon fell silent, when he finally spoke, his voice was barely a whisper. "I was ashamed of what Elisabeta made me do and what I became because of her. Even after centuries, just thinking about her fills me with fear." He looked up at Kate. His ancient eyes showed vulnerability in a way she hardly ever saw. "I didn't want you to know that part of me. The weak, broken part that still cowers at her memory."

Kate felt her anger falter in the face of his raw admission. "Devon, I've never expected you to be bulletproof. God knows I have my own traumas, my own weaknesses. What hurts is that you didn't trust me enough to share yours."

"It wasn't about trust," Devon said. "It was about pride. About wanting to be the strong one, a protector. About not wanting you to see me as I was with her, powerless and imprisoned."

Kate understood then why this particular lie had been so important to

Devon. His relationship with Elisabeta was a dark mirror of their own beginning, captor and captive, powerful and powerless. By hiding Elisabeta's existence, Devon had been trying to distance himself from an uncomfortable admission: That he had done to Kate what had once been done to him.

"We can't build a future on half-truths," Kate said finally. "I need to know that you'll be honest with me going forward, even when it's difficult. Even when it makes you vulnerable."

"I will," Devon promised. "No more secrets."

Kate nodded, accepting his words but not entirely ready to trust them. "So what do we do now? About Elisabeta?"

Devon seemed relieved by the shift to practical matters. "I've been in contact with Antoine and several other allies. They're gathering information, trying to figure out why she's chosen this moment to make contact."

"And in the meantime?"

"In the meantime, we take precautions. I can teach you mental techniques to resist her influence and block her ability to connect with your mind."

Kate considered this. "You think she'll try to contact me again? Like in the dream?"

"Yes," Devon said without hesitation. "The mirror created a connection. She'll use it."

"How?"

"Possibly to manipulate you. To satisfy her curiosity about what makes you special to me." Devon leaned forward, his expression intense. "Kate, you need to understand, Elisabeta is unlike anyone you've ever encountered. She's had eight centuries to perfect the art of psychological manipulation. She will find your vulnerabilities and exploit them without mercy."

Kate felt a chill at his words, but refused to show fear. "Tell me about these mental techniques."

For the next hour, Devon guided Kate through exercises designed to strengthen her mental barriers with visualization techniques, meditation practices, and methods for recognizing and resisting external influence. Kate was a quick study, her artist's imagination making it easy for her to create the mental shields Devon described.

"It's not foolproof," Devon cautioned as they finished. "Elisabeta is powerful, but these techniques will help you recognize her presence in your mind and resist her suggestions. Antoine is sending several trusted vampires to patrol the area. I'll need to feed more to maintain my strength." Devon paused. "And I'd prefer if you weren't alone, especially at night."

Kate bristled slightly at the last suggestion. "I'm not going to become a prisoner again, Devon. Not even for my own protection."

"That's not what I'm suggesting," Devon said quickly. "Just… reasonable precautions. The same you'd take if there were a human stalker or threat."

Kate considered this, then nodded reluctantly. "Fine. Reasonable precautions. But I'm not canceling my plans. I'm meeting Zoe tonight at a gallery opening. They're having a late-night exhibition that I promised I'd attend."

Devon tensed visibly. "Kate—"

"This isn't negotiable," she said firmly. "I'll take precautions. You can come with me. But I'm going."

Devon looked like he wanted to object further, but instead, he nodded stiffly. "Of course. We'll go together."

Kate could see the conflict in his eyes, the desire to protect her warring with his respect for her autonomy. It was a balance they were still learning to navigate, made all the more difficult by this new threat.

"Thank you," she said, softening slightly. "For respecting my decision."

Devon nodded again, but Kate could see that the tension hadn't left his body. Despite his words, he struggled with her choice. This only strengthened her resolve to keep her independence, even when faced with danger.

* * *

The gallery featured emerging artists working with light and shadow, installations that came alive in darkness, illuminated by strategic lighting that transformed the space into an otherworldly landscape.

Under normal circumstances, Kate would have been enthralled. Tonight, however, she was acutely aware of Devon beside her, his body tense with hyper vigilance as his eyes constantly scanned the crowded gallery.

"You're going to scare people if you keep looking like you expect an attack at any moment," Kate murmured, sipping her wine.

Devon made a visible effort to relax his posture. "Sorry," he said. "Old habits."

Kate spotted Zoe across the room, waving to catch her attention. Her roommate made her way through the crowd, her bright blue hair making her easy to track in the dimly lit space.

"Kate! You made it!" Zoe embraced her warmly. "What do you think of the exhibition? Mira's light sculpture is getting all the buzz."

Zoe led them through the gallery and pointed out pieces by artists they both knew. Kate was aware of the distance between herself and Devon. Normally, they would be close, with his hand on her lower back or her fingers linked with his. Tonight, she kept that small but significant space between them, a physical manifestation of her emotional withdrawal.

Devon noticed, of course he did, but made no attempt to bridge the gap. Instead, he followed slightly behind Kate and Zoe, his attention divided between their conversation and his constant surveillance of the gallery. Zoe glanced at Kate. "Is everything okay with you two?" she asked quietly once Devon stepped away to get Kate another drink.

Kate sighed. "It's complicated. We're working through some things."

"Want to talk about it?"

"Not right now," Kate said, watching Devon at the bar. Even from across the room, she could see his eyes constantly moving, scanning faces and looking for possible threats. "Maybe later."

Zoe nodded and respected her privacy. "You know where to find me if you need to vent or a place to crash."

Kate smiled in appreciation. "Thanks, Zo."

Devon returned with her wine.

"Thank you," she said, taking it without quite meeting his eyes.

The evening went on like this, with polite conversation and a careful distance. Devon's constant watchfulness created a feeling of tension that Kate couldn't shake. She became more and more irritated, both by his actions and by her own struggle to relax and enjoy the exhibition. When Zoe walked away to talk to another friend, Kate faced Devon. "You're making everyone uncomfortable," she said softly. "Including me."

Devon's jaw tightened. "I'm trying to keep you safe."

"No, you're hovering. There's a difference."

"Kate—"

"This is exactly what I was afraid of," she interrupted. "That we'd go right back to where we started, you controlling, me confined."

Devon flinched as if she'd struck him. "That's not my intention."

"Maybe not. But it's what's happening." Kate set down her wine glass. "I need some air."

Before Devon could respond, she walked away and headed for the gallery's small outdoor patio. The night air was cool against her flushed skin as she leaned against the railing, trying to calm her rising annoyance. Devon appeared beside her moments later, keeping a careful distance. "I'm sorry," he said quietly. "You're right. I'm being overbearing."

Kate sighed, her anger easing a bit. "I can't do this, Devon. I know you are scared, but I can't return to being watched and restricted all the time."

"I know, I'm trying to find a way to keep you safe while also respecting your freedom. It's just…" Devon paused, searching for the right words.

"Just what?"

"The thought of losing you frightens me," he admitted. "Not just to Elisabeta, but because of my own mistakes."

They stood in silence for a moment, the sounds of the gallery muted behind them. Finally, Kate broke the silence. "I think we should go back to the apartment. This isn't working tonight."

"Of course," Devon replied right away.

They said their goodbyes to Zoe, who shot Kate a worried look and whispered, "Call me tomorrow?" Kate nodded, promising to check in. The ride back home was quiet, both of them lost in their own thoughts. Kate stared out the window at the passing city lights, aware of Devon beside her but feeling miles apart. In the suite, the tension that had been building all evening finally erupted.

"This isn't working," Kate said, dropping her purse on the entry table with more force than necessary. "You, watching my every move, jumping at shadows, treating me like I'm made of glass."

Devon's careful composure cracked. "What would you have me do, Kate? Ignore the very real threat Elisabeta poses? Pretend everything is normal when we both know it isn't?"

"No, but there has to be a middle ground between ignoring the danger and… whatever this is." Kate gestured at him, at his rigid posture and vigilant eyes. "You're acting like you did when I first came to your estate, controlling and possessive."

"I'm trying to protect you!"

"I don't need your protection if it comes at the cost of my autonomy!" Kate's voice rose to match his. "We've been through this, Devon. We've had this exact conversation. I thought we were past it."

Devon ran a hand through his hair, a rare gesture of frustration. "This is different. Elisabeta isn't some abstract threat. She's real, she's dangerous, and she's fixated on you because of me."

"So what's your solution? Lock me away in your estate? Never let me out of your sight? That's not living, Devon. That's existing in a gilded cage, and I've already done that once."

The words hung between them, heavy with implication. Devon's face dropped, the parallel to their beginning clearly striking close to home.

"I'm not trying to cage you," he said, his voice softer now. "I'm trying to keep you alive."

"At what cost?" Kate asked. "My freedom? My sense of self? The trust we've built?" She shook her head. "I won't do it, Devon. I won't go back to that, not even for my safety."

Devon was quiet for a long moment, his eyes filled with conflict. "What do you want from me, Kate?" he finally asked. "Tell me what you need, and I'll try to give it to you."

Kate took a deep breath to gather her thoughts. "I need space," she said at last. "Time to process everything that's happened. Time to think about what it means for us and our future."

Devon went very still. "Space," he repeated, the word sounding foreign on his lips.

"Yes. A few days apart. I'll stay at Zoe's."

"Kate, that's not safe. If Elisabeta—"

"I'll take precautions," Kate interrupted. "I'll practice the mental techniques you taught me. I won't go out alone at night. But I need this, Devon. I need to step back and think clearly, without your fear and guilt influencing my every thought."

Devon looked stricken, but he didn't argue more. "If that's what you need," he said finally, his voice hollow.

"It is." Kate moved toward the bedroom to pack a bag, then paused. "This isn't about punishing you, Devon. It's about me needing space to sort through my feelings. To decide if I can trust you again."

Devon nodded once, his face a mask of careful control that didn't quite hide the pain in his eyes. "I understand."

Kate packed quickly, taking only what she needed for a few days. Devon watched from the doorway, his body unnaturally still in the way that reminded her he wasn't human, had never been human in all the time she'd known him.

When she was finished, she turned to face him. "I'll call you," she promised. "And I'll be careful."

Devon nodded again, not trusting himself to speak.

Kate moved past him, bag in hand, then stopped. Despite everything, she couldn't leave like this, with so much unsaid between them. She set down her bag and turned back to him. "I still love you," she said softly. "I'm angry and hurt, but I still love you, that hasn't changed. I just need time."

Devon's composure cracked then, his face revealing a vulnerability that few had ever witnessed. "I love you too," he said, the words still new enough to sound strange in his voice. "More than I thought possible."

Kate stepped forward and kissed him briefly, a gentle press of lips that carried both promise and farewell. Then she picked up her bag and walked to the door. "Kate," Devon called as she reached for the handle. She turned back to look at him. "Be safe," he said simply.

"I will."

The door closed behind her with a soft click that seemed to echo in the sudden silence of the suite. Devon stood motionless, listening to her footsteps retreat down the hallway, the ding of the elevator, the final moment when she passed beyond even his enhanced hearing. He moved to the window and looked out at the city. He couldn't stand the idea that she was out there somewhere, away from his protection. But he would put up with it for her sake, because she had asked. Despite all his instincts telling him to follow her and keep her safe. Even if it meant facing his biggest fear, that by trying to protect her from Elisabeta, he might still lose her.

* * *

The familiar scent of oil paint and turpentine greeted her as Zoe unlocked the door and ushered her inside. "Your corner is just like you left it," Zoe said, gesturing to the area that had been Kate's bedroom and workspace before Budapest. "I haven't touched anything except when I clean around the place."

Kate set her bag down, looking around with a strange sense of dislocation. While it had only been months since she lived here, it felt like a lifetime ago. "Thanks for letting me crash," Kate said as she sank onto the futon that had been her bed. "I know it's sudden."

"Hey, it's still your home too," Zoe said, sitting beside her. "Want to talk about it now?"

Kate sighed, trying to formulate a version of the truth that didn't involve vampires and ancient makers. "Devon lied to me," she said finally. "About something important from his past. Something that's affecting us now."

Zoe nodded, not pressing for details. "And you needed space to think."

"Yeah. It's complicated. He had reasons for keeping it from me, not good reasons, but I understand them. But trust is..." Kate trailed off, searching for words.

"Essential," Zoe finished for her. "Especially after what happened with Jason."

"Exactly," Kate agreed. "Devon knows how important honesty and trust are to me, which makes this lie even worse."

"Do you think you can forgive him?"

Kate thought about it for a moment. "I think so, with time. But I need to be sure I'm forgiving him because I'm certain we have a future together, not because I'm afraid of losing what we have."

Zoe squeezed her hand. "That's wise. And very mature."

Kate smiled wryly. "I'm trying. It's not easy."

They caught up over the next hour. Zoe shared updates from their friendship circle while skillfully avoiding more questions about Devon. Kate appreciated Zoe's knack for knowing when to let things go. She started to feel tired, so she decided to call it a night. The emotional toll of the past twenty-four hours, combined with her disrupted sleep the night before, left Kate barely able to keep her eyes open.

"Get some rest," Zoe said, noticing her fatigue. "We can talk more tomorrow."

Kate nodded gratefully and got ready for bed in the familiar yet strange bathroom. As she brushed her teeth, she listened for Devon's movements. This habit had developed over months of living together. The silence she encountered felt both freeing and isolating. Back on her futon, Kate checked her phone.

Three text messages from Devon:

Did you arrive safely?

Please let me know you're alright.

I respect your need for space. Just confirm you're safe and I won't contact you again until you're ready.

The progression from concern to acceptance made Kate's heart ache. She typed a quick reply:

I'm at Zoe's. Safe. Will call in a few days.

His response came immediately:

Thank you. Be careful. I love you.

Kate set the phone aside without replying to his last message. She turned off the light and lay in the darkness, listening to the sounds of the city outside, Zoe moving around in her room, the hum of the refrigerator, the distant wail of sirens that was the constant soundtrack of New York nights.

Sleep came slowly, as her mind replayed the events of the past two days repeatedly. She finally drifted off into restless dreams, beneath them a presence, watching and waiting with endless patience. Kate woke suddenly, her heart racing, the feeling of being watched still clinging to her. Zoe's gentle snoring coming through the thin wall that separated their spaces, nothing seemed out of place, and yet…

Kate reached for her phone, her finger hovering over Devon's name. She wanted to call him, to hear his voice and be reassured by his presence. But that would defeat the purpose of this time apart. She needed to stand on her own, face her fears without running back to Devon at the first sign of trouble.

She set the phone down and lay back, staring at the ceiling. "I know you're there," she whispered into the darkness. "I'm not afraid of you."

No one responded. Kate hadn't expected a reply. This was a test of patience and mental strategy. Elisabeta had centuries of experience, but Kate had something the ancient vampire couldn't grasp. She had the strength that comes from choosing love over fear and trust over control.

She would need all the strength she could muster to work through her complicated feelings for Devon and face the threat from his past. Whatever came next, she would face it on her own terms.

Chapter 11

Devon stood still at the window long after Kate had left. The city stretched out before him, filled with thousands of lights, each representing different lives. Among them was the one person who meant more to him than anything else. His phone buzzed. It was a text from Richard, his security chief.

"Package delivered to Miss Morgan's location. Team in position."

Guilt washed over Devon, sharp and acidic. Kate had asked for space and trust; he was offering neither. Leaving her unprotected with Elisabeta circling was unthinkable, but the surveillance team was a distant, impersonal betrayal. The pendant was not. His mother's moonstone, resting against Kate's skin, was a symbol of his love. And a lie. She had no idea the delicate silver contained a tracker. He told himself it was to keep her safe, but a harsher truth whispered that he couldn't bear to lose her. An invisible leash that he justified as a lifeline.

He quickly typed back:

"Maintain distance. She must not know. Report only if there's immediate danger."

Devon set the phone down and moved to his study, where he poured himself a glass of blood from his private reserve. The liquid was cold, lacking the warmth and vitality of fresh feeding, but it would sustain him. Everything felt cold now, without Kate's presence to warm the spaces between his ribs where something resembling a heart still beat.

The apartment felt empty without her. He missed her laughter and the way she gently teased him about his old-fashioned mannerisms. Her art supplies, scattered across the dining table, seemed to mock him with their neglect. Devon walked over to the table and carefully picked up her pencils, putting them back in the wooden box she liked.

Her sketchbook lay open to a drawing of him reading, captured in profile with an expression of contentment she'd somehow managed to convey with just a few precise lines. He traced the edge of the paper with one finger, remembering the evening she'd drawn it, how she'd insisted he stay perfectly still while she worked, how she'd bitten her gorgeous, plump lower lip in concentration.

His phone rang, jarring him from his thoughts. Antoine's name appeared on the screen.

"I heard," Antoine said without preamble when Devon answered. "Richard contacted me about the security arrangements."

"She needed space," Devon said, his voice carefully neutral. "I'm respecting that."

"While having her followed by a team of professionals."

"I won't apologize for making sure she is safe."

Antoine was quiet for a moment. "You know this could backfire spectacularly if she finds out."

"She won't find out because she trusts me to respect her wishes," Devon interrupted, then immediately regretted the bitter irony in his own words.

"Ah," Antoine said softly. "And there's the crux of it. You're using her trust in your honesty to deceive her about your protective measures."

Devon closed his eyes, the truth of Antoine's words hitting him like a physical blow. "What would you have me do? Leave her completely vulnerable?"

"I would have you consider that Kate is stronger and more resilient than you think. That perhaps your need to protect her says more about your own fears than about any real danger she faces."

"Elisabeta is not a figment of my imagination, Antoine. The threat is real."

"Yes, but Kate handled it when Elisabeta contacted her directly. She recognized the threat, told you about it, and she's taking precautions. She's not helpless, Devon."

Devon was silent, unable to answer because he wasn't sure himself. Where did legitimate concern end and paranoid overprotection begin? "You're right," he said quietly.

"I often am," Antoine replied with gentle humor. "The question is, what are you going to do about it?"

Devon looked out at the city again, thinking of Kate somewhere out there, trying to process her feelings about his deception while remaining unaware of the larger deceptions still surrounding her. "I'm going to trust her," he said finally. "Really trust her. With the entire truth."

"Even if that means pulling back your security team?"

Devon's jaw tightened. "Let's not get ahead of ourselves. I said I was going to trust her, not that I was going to be reckless with her life."

Antoine chuckled. "Small steps, then. But steps in the right direction." After they hung up, Devon remained at the window until the first hint of dawn began to creep in. As his body began to enter dormancy, he made a decision. When Kate was ready to talk, he would tell her everything. He would give her all the information she needed to make truly informed choices about her own safety and their future together.

Devon's last conscious thought before sleep took him was a prayer to whatever gods might listen to creatures like him: Let her forgive me. Let her choose us. Let her be safe.

Somewhere across the city, Kate lay awake staring up at Zoe's ceiling. She wondered if she'd made the right choice in leaving, oblivious to the fact that she was still being watched over by the man she was trying to learn to trust again.

Chapter 12

The familiar sound of Zoe's coffee grinder woke Kate. She lay still on the futon for a moment as she got used to her old life's morning routine. The light streaming through the apartment's large windows felt harsh. The sounds of the city, with traffic, construction, and the general chaos of New York waking up, felt overwhelming.

"Morning, sunshine," Zoe called from the kitchen. "Coffee's almost ready."

Kate forced a smile as she padded across the apartment. "Thanks. I didn't realize how much I missed your industrial-strength brew."

Zoe appeared in the doorway, holding two steaming mugs. She was already dressed for the day in paint-splattered jeans and a vintage Ramones band t-shirt, her blue hair pulled back in a messy bun. "You look like shit," she stated with characteristic bluntness.

"Feel like it too." Kate gratefully accepted the coffee, wrapping her hands around the warm ceramic. "I forgot how loud the city is in the morning."

"You've been living in a bubble," Zoe said, settling into the chair across from her. "Literally. That penthouse of his might as well be on another planet." Kate nodded, taking a sip of coffee. "Want to come with me to the studio today?" Zoe asked. "Might be good to get your hands dirty again. Remember what it feels like to create something."

Kate considered this. She hadn't painted anything in a while. "Yeah," she said, surprising herself with the decisiveness in her voice. "I'd like that."

* * *

The art collective in Gowanus that morning was energetic and filled with the controlled chaos of a dozen artists working on their individual projects. The familiar smell of anise oil and paint hit her as soon as they walked in, and for the first time since leaving Devon's apartment, Kate felt something loosen in her chest.

"Kate!" Tony, a sculptor who worked in the corner space, looked up from his latest piece. "Where the hell have you been? We thought you'd been abducted by aliens or something."

"Something like that," Kate replied, managing a smile. Her easel was still there, covered with a paint-stained cloth. Zoe had been maintaining her space, keeping her supplies organized and her canvases safe. Kate pulled away the cloth to look at her last painting, an abstract piece in blues and greys that she had been working on before everything changed. With fresh eyes, the painting lacked soul. She noticed the careful brushstrokes and the thoughtful composition, but it had no passion. There was no risk.

"You've changed," Zoe observed, watching Kate study her own work.

"Have I?"

"Your whole energy is different. More… intense. Like you've been living at a higher frequency."

Kate picked up a brush, testing its weight in her hand. "Maybe I have been." She spent the morning working on the canvas, letting her hands move without conscious direction. Colors emerged. deep crimsons and midnight blues, touches of silver that caught the light. She wasn't sure what she was painting, but it just felt necessary to get it out onto canvas. Around noon, she received a text from an unknown number:

Hope you're having a good day. - M

Kate frowned at the message, confused. She didn't know anyone with the initial M who would be texting her. She was about to delete it when something made her pause. The timing felt strange with everything else happening in her life right now.

"You okay?" Zoe asked as she noticed Kate's expression.

"Weird text from someone I don't know," Kate replied, showing her the phone.

Zoe read it. "Probably spam. I get those all the time."

Kate nodded, but something about the message bothered her. She deleted it and tried to focus on her painting, the unease lingered. That afternoon, Kate went out alone for the first time since leaving Devon. She needed basic items like shampoo and toothpaste that she had become used to having provided for her. Making a shopping list felt very ordinary compared to the life she had lived for the past few months.

The corner bodega was busy with the usual late-afternoon rush of people grabbing snacks and drinks. Kate moved through the aisles, filling her basket with necessities, when she noticed him. A man in a dark jacket, standing by the magazine rack, not really reading anything. He'd been behind her in line at the coffee shop that morning, she realized. And now here he was again.

Kate paid for her items, her instincts on edge. As she left the store, she spied the man speaking quietly into what looked like a Bluetooth earpiece. Her blood ran cold. Kate walked quickly toward the subway station, her mind racing. Was she being paranoid? Or was someone actually following her?

At the subway entrance, she paused and looked back. The man was nowhere to be seen, but that didn't make her feel better. If someone was professional enough to tail her, they'd be professional enough to stay hidden when she was looking for them. On the train back to Zoe's apartment, Kate's phone buzzed again. Another text from the same unknown number:

Glad to see you're being careful. Stay safe.

Kate's hands shook as she read the message. Someone was definitely watching her, but who? And why were they texting her about it? Unless… A horrible thought occurred to her. What if Devon had hired someone to watch her? What if his promise to respect her space was just another lie?

The thought made her sick. After everything they'd discussed, her specific request for space, would he really step over that line? Kate stared at the phone, debating whether to call him later that night and confront him directly. But if she was wrong, if the surveillance wasn't his, then calling him would only prove that she couldn't handle being on her own. And if she was right…

If she was right, then everything she'd feared about their relationship was true. Back at Zoe's apartment that evening, Kate tried to act normal, but her friend picked up on her agitation immediately.

"What's wrong?" Zoe asked, looking up from her laptop where she was editing photos of her latest installation.

Kate hesitated, then decided she needed to tell someone. "I think I'm being followed."

Zoe's eyebrows shot up. "Followed? By who?"

"I don't know. Maybe… maybe Devon hired someone to watch me."

"That bastard," Zoe said immediately. "After everything you told him about needing space?"

"I don't know for sure it's him," Kate said quickly, though her heart wasn't in the defense. "It could be someone else."

"Who else would have you followed? Kate, this is exactly the kind of controlling behavior you were trying to get away from."

Kate sank onto the couch, feeling defeated. "I know. I just… I wanted to believe he'd changed. That he could respect my boundaries."

Zoe moved to sit beside her, her expression softening. "Maybe he has changed, and this is just his way of trying to protect you without interfering directly. Guys can be really stupid about this stuff, especially guys who are used to being in control."

"That doesn't make it okay."

"No, it doesn't. But it might make it understandable."

Kate's phone buzzed again. This time, it was a call from Devon himself. Kate stared at the screen, her thumb hovering over the answer button.

"You don't have to talk to him if you're not ready," Zoe said softly.

Kate let the call go to voicemail, but she quickly felt guilty. A few minutes later, her phone pinged with a new voicemail. She played the message on speaker so Zoe could listen.

"Kate, it's me. I know you asked for space. I'm trying to respect that, but I needed to hear your voice. To know you're okay. I… I miss you. I know I made mistakes, and I know you need time to process everything, but I want you to know that I'm here when you're ready to talk. I love you."

His voice was soft, vulnerable in a way that made Kate's chest ache. This was the Devon she'd fallen in love with, not the controlling vampire aristocrat, but the man who'd learned to open his heart after centuries of isolation.

"He sounds miserable," Zoe observed.

"Good," Kate said, but there was no real venom in it. "He should feel miserable. He lied to me."

"Yeah, he did. But he also sounds like he knows he screwed up."

Kate looked at her friend. "Whose side are you on?"

"Yours, always. But that doesn't mean I can't see that you're miserable too."

Kate couldn't deny it. She was miserable. Her life felt empty without Devon's presence, too small and too bright and too loud. She kept reaching for her phone to share random thoughts with him, kept turning to speak to him, only to remember he wasn't there.

"I feel like half of myself is missing," she admitted quietly. "Like I'm hollow without him."

"Sounds like love," Zoe said. "It makes you feel incomplete when the other person isn't there. The question is whether that feeling is worth the complications that come with him."

Kate thought about this as she got ready for bed later that night. Was the feeling of incompleteness a sign of unhealthy dependence, or was it simply what it felt like to love someone so deeply that they became part of your essential self? Being with Devon had awakened parts of herself she'd never known were there, not just as an artist, but as a woman, someone capable of the kind of love that transformed you completely.

But it had also made her dependent in ways that scared her. As she lay in the darkness, listening to the sounds of the city that never slept, Kate tried to picture her future. Could she return to her old life and pretend that Devon had never existed? The idea made her feel like she would be a ghost of her former self.

But could she go back to him without losing who she was? Could they find a balance between love and independence, protection and freedom? Her phone lit up with another text from an unknown number:

Sweet dreams.

Kate's heart pounded as she looked at the message. Someone was definitely watching her, and they were close enough to know when she went to bed. If Devon was behind this, then he hadn't learned anything from their fight. He was still the same controlling creature who had kept her captive, just with better PR. But what if it wasn't Devon? What if someone else was watching her...

Kate thought of Elisabeta, of the woman in the mirror with her terrible smile. Was this her game? Messing with her head to make her feel unsafe, to drive her back to Devon's protection? Either way, Kate was tired of being a passive player in other people's games. Tomorrow, she would find out who was watching her and why.

And then she would decide what to do about Devon. Drifting off to sleep, Kate's last conscious thought was a resolution: She would not be anyone's Pet, possession, or victim. Not Devon's, not Elisabeta's, not anyone's.

She was Kate Morgan, and she was nobody's pawn.

Chapter 13

Kate woke the next morning with a plan of action and a sense of purpose she hadn't felt in days. The anger that had been simmering beneath her hurt and confusion had transformed into determination. She would not spend another day wondering who was watching her or why.

"You look different," Zoe observed over breakfast. "More… focused."

"I'm done being a victim," Kate said as she stirred her coffee with unnecessary force. "If someone wants to play games with me, they're going to find out I'm not as helpless as they think."

Zoe raised an eyebrow. "What's the plan?"

"I'm going to flush them out. Make them show themselves."

"Kate, that sounds dangerous—"

"Everything about my life is dangerous now," Kate interrupted. "At least this way, I'm choosing the terms."

She spent the morning preparing. If someone was watching her, they'd expect her to follow her routine from yesterday. Instead, she would do something unexpected, something that would force them to react. Kate dressed carefully in jeans, sneakers, and a jacket with multiple pockets. She put her phone on silent and slipped it into her back pocket, then grabbed her sketchbook and a few pencils. To anyone watching, she would look like she was heading out for a casual day of drawing in the city.

"Be careful," Zoe said as Kate headed for the door. "And call me if anything weird happens."

"I will."

Kate left the apartment that afternoon and walked toward the subway, but instead of going down to the platform, she ducked into a coffee shop across the street. From the window, she had a clear view of the apartment building and the surrounding street. She didn't have to wait long.

A man in a dark jacket, the same one from yesterday, she was almost certain, emerged from a doorway down the block. He looked around, clearly searching for her, then pulled out his phone and made a call. Kate's heart pounded as she watched him. He was definitely following her, and he was definitely professional. The way he moved, the way he scanned the area, the calm efficiency with which he handled her disappearance, this wasn't some random stalker.

This was someone who'd been hired to watch her.

The man finished his call and began walking in her direction. Kate quickly paid for her coffee and slipped out the back exit of the shop, emerging onto a side street. She had a plan now, but it required getting to a specific location without being seen. For the rest of the day, Kate led her tail on a winding route through Manhattan, using every trick she could think of to stay ahead of him. She ducked through department stores, used multiple subway entrances, and doubled back on herself several times. It was exhausting, but also exciting. For the first time in days, she felt like herself again, resourceful, independent, and in control.

By evening, she made her way to Times Square, one of the most crowded places in the city. If she was going to confront her watcher, she wanted to do it somewhere public, somewhere safe. Kate positioned herself near the red steps, her back to a wall so no one could approach her from behind. She pulled out her sketchbook and pretended to draw, but her eyes were constantly scanning the crowd.

It took twenty minutes, but eventually she spotted him. He was trying to blend in with the tourists, but his constant attention to his phone and his systematic scanning of the area gave him away. Kate stood up and began walking directly toward him. The man noticed her approach and immediately turned away, but Kate was done playing games.

"Excuse me," she called out loudly enough to attract attention from nearby tourists. "I think you dropped something."

The man had no choice but to turn around. Up close, Kate could see he was probably in his thirties, fit, with the kind of alert eyes that suggested a military or law enforcement background.

"I'm sorry?" he said, his voice carefully neutral.

"You've been following me for two days," Kate said, keeping her voice conversational but loud enough that people around them could hear. "I'm wondering if you'd like to explain why."

The man's expression didn't change, but Kate saw his hand move slightly toward his jacket. "I think you're mistaken, miss."

"Am I? Because I have a very good memory for faces, and yours has been showing up everywhere I go." Kate pulled out her phone. "Should I call the police and let them sort it out?"

For a moment, they stared at each other. Kate could see the man calculating his options, weighing his orders against the very public scene she was creating. Finally, he sighed. "Miss Morgan, I think we should have a conversation. Somewhere more private."

"I'm not going anywhere private with you," Kate said firmly. "But I'll listen to what you have to say right here."

The man looked around at the growing crowd of curious onlookers, then back at Kate. "My name is Richard Chen. I work for a private security firm. I've been hired to ensure your safety."

"Hired by who?"

Richard hesitated. "I think you already know the answer to that."

Kate felt a surge of anger so intense it made her dizzy. "Devon."

"Mr Karlov was concerned about your welfare. Given the recent threats—"

"Stop," Kate said, holding up a hand. "Just stop talking."

She turned and walked away, pushing through the crowd with Richard calling after her. But she didn't stop, didn't look back, didn't slow down until she was several blocks away and certain she'd lost him in the chaos of the city. Only then did she pull out her phone and call Devon. He answered on the first ring.

"Kate? Are you alright? Richard said—"

"You son of a bitch," Kate said, her voice shaking with fury. "You lying, controlling son of a bitch."

There was silence on the other end of the line.

"I asked for space," Kate continued, not caring that people on the street were staring at her. "I asked for trust. And you hired someone to follow me?"

"Kate, please let me explain—"

"Explain what? How you decided that my explicit request was just a suggestion? How you thought it was okay to have me watched like a criminal while pretending to respect my wishes?"

"I was trying to protect you—"

"No!" Kate's voice cracked. "You were trying to control me. Just like always. You can't help yourself, can you? You can't stand the idea that I might be able to take care of myself."

"Kate, that's not true. I know you're strong—"

"Then why?" Kate demanded. "Why couldn't you just trust me? Why couldn't you believe that I could handle a few days on my own without your protection?"

Devon was quiet for a long moment. When he spoke again, his voice was soft, defeated. "Because I'm terrified," he admitted. "Because the thought of something happening to you while you're angry with me, while we're apart... I couldn't bear it."

Kate felt tears threatening, but she pushed them back, brushing away a few strays with the back of her hand. "So you decided to lie to me. Again."

"I didn't lie—"

"You let me believe I was free when I wasn't. You let me think you were respecting my wishes when you weren't. That's lying, Devon."

"You're right," Devon said quietly. "You're absolutely right. I'm sorry."

"Sorry doesn't fix this," Kate said. "Sorry doesn't undo the fact that you can't trust me to make my own decisions."

"Kate, please—"

"I need more time," Kate said, cutting him off. "I mean it. No more tails, no protection. If you can't respect that, if you can't trust me to take care of myself, then we don't have a future together."

"Kate—"

She hung up before he could say anything else. Kate stood on the busy street corner, people flowing around her like water around a stone, and felt more alone than she had since the day she'd first woken up in Devon's estate. But it was a different kind of alone, not the helpless isolation of captivity; it was the fierce solitude of someone standing on her own two feet.

Her phone immediately started ringing again. Devon's name flashed on the screen, but Kate declined the call. It rang again, and again she declined it. After the fourth attempt, she turned the phone off entirely. She needed to think, and she couldn't do that with Devon's voice in her ear.

Kate began walking, not caring where she was going, just needing to move. The city blurred around her as she processed what had just happened. Devon had hired someone to watch her. Despite everything they'd discussed, he'd decided he knew better than she did about her own safety.

The betrayal cut deeper than his lie about Elisabeta, because this wasn't about his past; this was about his fundamental inability to see her as capable. This was about his conviction that she was too weak, too human, too fragile to be trusted with her own life.

Kate walked to Central Park and sat on a bench by the reservoir. She took a breath and tried to calm down. A jogger went past, followed by another. Regular people living ordinary lives, oblivious to the existence of vampires and ancient beings toying with human hearts. Kate envied their ignorance.

Her phone buzzed in her pocket, a text message that had come through before she'd turned it off. She almost ignored it, but something made her check. It wasn't from Devon. It was from the unknown number that had been texting her:

Well done. You're stronger than he gives you credit for.

Kate stared at the message, her blood running cold. Someone else had been watching her confrontation with Richard. Someone who wasn't part of Devon's security team. Another message appeared:

He'll never see you as his equal. You know this now.

Kate's hands shook as she read the words. This wasn't Devon's doing. This was someone else, someone who'd been watching her, studying her, learning her weaknesses.

Elisabeta.

Of course, this was all her plan. Isolate Kate from Devon, create distance between them, and take advantage of their existing tensions and insecurities. Kate stood up suddenly and looked around the park carefully. Elisabeta was here, somewhere, watching her. The ancient vampire had orchestrated this entire confrontation, had probably been feeding suspicions into Kate's head about being followed, and had manipulated her into discovering Devon's security detail at exactly the right moment to cause maximum damage to their relationship. And Kate had played right into her hands.

She turned her phone back on and immediately called Devon. This time, he answered before the first ring finished.

"Kate, thank God. I was so worried—"

"Devon, listen to me," Kate interrupted. "I'm in Central Park, near the reservoir. I think Elisabeta is here. I think she's been manipulating this whole situation."

"What? Kate, get out of there. Now."

"I'm going to, but you need to know that she's been texting me. Watching me. She set me up to discover your security team."

"I'm coming to get you—"

"No," Kate said firmly. "Send Richard. I'll wait for him by the park entrance on Fifth Avenue. But Devon?"

"Yes?"

"We still need to talk. About everything. The security, the lying, all of it. This doesn't change what happened between us."

"I know," Devon said quietly. "I know we do. But first, let's get you somewhere safe."

Kate began walking quickly toward the park exit, her eyes scanning the crowds for any sign of the beautiful, terrible woman from the mirror. "I'm scared," she admitted.

"I know. But you're also brave, and you're smart, and you just figured out a game that's been playing for days. You're going to be okay."

"How do you know?"

"Because," Devon said, and she could hear the smile in his voice despite everything, "you're Kate Morgan. And Kate Morgan doesn't let anyone, vampire or human, tell her what she can and cannot do."

Despite everything, Kate found herself smiling too. "Damn right I don't."

She spotted Richard waiting by a black sedan when she reached the park entrance. It was then that Kate realized something important: She was angry with Devon, hurt by his deception, frustrated by his inability to trust her judgment. But she wasn't ready to give up on them. Not yet.

And certainly not because some ancient vampire thought she could manipulate Kate into abandoning the man she loved. If Elisabeta wanted a fight, she'd get one.

Chapter 14

A day had passed since Kate's escape from Central Park. Devon watched as the city lights emerged with the setting of dusk over New York. He was frozen between action and restraint, between his desperate need to protect Kate and his respect for her request for space. He barely heard the knock at the door, only registering it when it became more insistent. Devon moved to answer it, already knowing who stood on the other side.

"Antoine," he said, stepping back to allow the other vampire entry.

Antoine, once a Roman centurion, was now a sleek businessman in an impeccable suit. He nodded as he entered. "Devon. You look terrible."

"Thank you for coming," Devon said, ignoring the observation.

"Of course." Antoine moved into the suite, his dark eyes taking in the space. "Are you alright?"

"Yes. For now."

Antoine nodded, understanding without judgment. "So now you're torn between respecting her wishes and protecting her from a threat she can't possibly understand."

Devon turned away, unable to maintain his composure under his friend's perceptive gaze. "What have you learned?"

Antoine accepted the change of subject gracefully. "Elisabeta has been in New York for at least a week. She's established a temporary residence in a townhouse on the Upper East Side. She's brought three of her progeny with her: Nikolai, Siobhan, and a new one I don't recognize."

Devon absorbed this information with growing dread. "A full entourage.

This isn't a casual visit."

"No," Antoine agreed. "This is deliberate. Planned."

"Why now?" Devon asked, more to himself than to Antoine. "She's left me alone for decades at a time. Why suddenly take an interest in Kate?"

Antoine settled into an armchair, his posture relaxed but his eyes alert. "Perhaps because Kate is different. In all the centuries I've known you, Devon, I've never seen you form an attachment like this. Not to a human, not to anyone."

Devon couldn't deny it. In his entire existence, Kate was unique, the only being who had truly breached the walls around his heart, who had made him feel human again in ways he'd thought lost forever. Devon ran a hand through his hair, a human gesture of frustration he'd never quite abandoned. "I need to warn Kate."

"She asked for space," Antoine reminded him gently.

After Antoine left, Devon sank onto the sofa, his body heavy with worry. Somewhere out there, Kate was alone, vulnerable to a threat she couldn't possibly understand. For the first time in centuries, Devon felt truly helpless. Not even Elisabeta's decades of torment had left him feeling this vulnerable or exposed. Because now he had something to lose that mattered more than his own existence.

He had Kate. Or at least, he had the hope of Kate, if he could find a way to regain her trust. And he would do anything, respect any boundary, face any fear, to keep that hope alive.

* * *

Kate stared at the invitation in her hand, turning it over as if the elegant cream cardstock might reveal hidden secrets. It had arrived by courier an hour ago, addressed specifically to her at Zoe's apartment, an address she hadn't shared with anyone since arriving.

"What is it?" Zoe asked, peering over her shoulder.

"An invitation to a gallery opening," Kate said, still studying the handwritten script. "Tonight at midnight. Some place called Galerie Nocturn."

"Midnight?" Zoe raised an eyebrow. "That's weird."

"Yeah." Kate turned the invitation over again. No return address, no contact information, just the gallery's name and address in the East Village, and the time: 12:00 AM.

"Are you going to go?" Zoe asked.

Kate hesitated. Her instincts screamed that this was connected to Elisabeta somehow. Which was precisely why a part of her wanted to go. To face this threat directly rather than hiding, waiting for it to find her.

"I think I might," she said finally.

"Want company?" Zoe offered. "I don't have plans tonight."

Kate considered it. Having Zoe with her would provide some security, a witness, if nothing else. But it would also put her friend in potential danger.

"Thanks, but I think I need to do this alone," she said. "It's probably just some pretentious art thing. You know how the scene can be, always trying to be edgy with weird hours and exclusive guest lists."

Zoe didn't look convinced. "If you're sure. But text me when you get there, okay? And when you leave."

"Yes, mom," Kate teased, trying to lighten the mood.

After Zoe left for her evening yoga class, Kate sat with the invitation, debating. The rational part of her knew she should call Devon, tell him about it, maybe even ask him to accompany her. But the part of her still raw from his deception resisted. She needed to prove, to herself as much as to him, that she could handle this situation independently. Still, she wasn't foolish. She took out her phone and sent Devon a text:

Received invitation to midnight gallery opening at Galerie Nocturn in East Village. Going to check it out. Just so you know where I am.

His response came almost immediately:

Don't go. It's a trap.

Kate stared at the three words, feeling a surge of irritation. No explanation, no offer to discuss it, just a command. As if she were a Pet, to be directed and controlled.

Thanks for the concern, but I can make my own decisions.

She sent the text before she could reconsider, then turned off her phone. She knew she was being petty, possibly even reckless, but Devon's high-handed approach had triggered all her old resentments about their power imbalance.

Kate spent the next few hours getting ready, both mentally and physically. She practiced the shielding techniques Devon had taught her to strengthen her mental barriers. She chose her outfit carefully. She picked practical boots that would allow her to run if needed, and layered clothing for freedom of movement.

By the time she left the apartment, Kate had almost convinced herself that the invitation was innocent, perhaps from someone at the collective who had heard she was back in town, or from her former gallery trying to reconnect. Almost, but not quite. The taxi dropped her off in front of a narrow townhouse in the East Village, its facade unmarked except for a small brass plaque reading "Galerie Nocturn" beside the door. The windows were covered with heavy drapes, allowing only the faintest hint of light to escape.

Kate checked her watch: 11:58 PM. She took a deep breath, centering herself, then climbed the steps and knocked on the door. It opened immediately to show a tall, pale man in a sharp suit. "Ms Morgan," he said with an Eastern European accent. "We've been expecting you. Please, come in." Kate hesitated, every instinct warning her to run in the opposite direction. But she had come too far; turning back now would change nothing. She stepped inside.

The gallery was dimly lit, the walls painted a deep burgundy that absorbed what little light there was. Artwork hung at carefully spaced intervals, paintings and photographs that Kate couldn't quite make out in the low light. Classical music played softly from hidden speakers.

"May I take your coat?" the man asked.

"No, thank you," Kate said, keeping it on like armor. "I tend to get cold."

He nodded, unperturbed. "Of course. Please, explore at your leisure. The other guests are already here."

Kate moved deeper into the gallery, her eyes adjusting to the darkness. She could make out perhaps a dozen other people scattered throughout the space, all elegantly dressed, all unnaturally still as they contemplated the artwork. All vampires, she realized with a sinking feeling. Devon had been right. This was a trap. She turned toward the exit, trying to appear casual, only to find her path blocked by two women who hadn't been there a moment before. They smiled at her with identical expressions of polite interest that didn't reach their eyes.

"Leaving so soon?" one asked. "But you haven't even seen the main exhibition."

Kate forced herself to remain calm. "Actually, I just remembered another commitment. If you'll excuse me—"

"The artist would be so disappointed," the other woman said, her voice a musical lilt. "She's been looking forward to meeting you."

Kate reached for her phone, only to find no signal. Of course.

"I really must insist," the first woman said, her smile widening to reveal the tips of delicate fangs. "It would be terribly rude to leave without greeting your hostess."

Kate knew she was trapped. Even if she could somehow get past these two, there were others between her and the door, all with supernatural speed and strength.

"Fine," she said, straightening her spine. "Lead the way."

The women flanked her, guiding her toward a door at the back of the gallery. Kate inspected the artwork more closely as they walked. Each piece showed scenes of captivity and freedom. Birds in cages with open doors, people standing at thresholds. The symbolism wasn't subtle.

The door opened into a small, intimate room furnished like a Victorian parlor with velvet settees, an ornate side table, and a crystal chandelier casting prismatic light over everything. Seated in a high-backed chair, like a queen holding court, was Elisabeta.

In person, she was even more striking than in Kate's dream. Ageless beauty combined with an aura of power that seemed to fill the room. She wore a simple black cocktail dress that emphasized her pale skin and dark hair, her only adornment a silver pendant that Kate recognized with a shock, the same family crest that had been engraved on the mirror.

"Katherine Morgan," Elisabeta said, her voice like warm honey. "How lovely of you to accept my invitation."

Kate remained in the doorway, unwilling to step further into what felt like a lion's den. "I don't recall your name being on it."

Elisabeta laughed, the sound musical and strangely compelling. "Direct. I appreciate that in a human. Please, sit." She gestured to a settee across from her chair.

Kate stayed where she was. "I prefer to stand."

"As you wish." Elisabeta studied her with open curiosity. "You're afraid, but controlling it well. Impressive."

"What do you want?" Kate asked, seeing no point in pretence.

"To meet you, of course. The human who has so thoroughly captivated my creation." Elisabeta leaned forward slightly. "I've been watching Devon for centuries, you know. He's had his diversions, his obsessions. But never has he risked so much for a mere mortal."

"If you've been watching him for centuries, why make contact now?" Kate asked, trying to understand the vampire's motives.

"Because now is when it became interesting." Elisabeta rose with fluid grace, moving to examine a painting on the wall, one of Kate's own works, she realized with a jolt. It was a piece she'd created at Devon's estate, a self-portrait of sorts showing a woman half in shadow, half in light. Elisabeta must have purchased it from the Whitespace gallery exhibition.

"You've changed him," Elisabeta continued, tracing the edge of the canvas with one pale finger. "In ways I wouldn't have thought possible after centuries. It's… fascinating."

"I haven't changed him," Kate said. "I just see him for who he is, beneath the mask he wears."

Elisabeta turned to her, head tilted in a gesture that reminded Kate uncomfortably of Devon. "Is that what you believe? That you know the 'real' Devon?" Her smile was pitying. "My dear, I created him. I know every part of him, the darkness he tries to hide, every weakness he pretends doesn't exist." Kate felt doubt creeping into her mind, like cold fingers touching her confidence. She recognized the feeling from her dream, where Elisabeta tried to influence her thoughts. She reinforced her mental shields, imagining them as walls of light around her mind.

"If you know him so well, why did he leave you?"

Something flashed in Elisabeta's eyes, anger, or maybe surprise at Kate's directness. "He didn't leave me. I released him when he no longer amused me."

"That's not how he tells it," Kate said, pressing the advantage. "He says he escaped during a fire. That you kept him prisoner for fifty years."

"Is that what he told you?" Elisabeta laughed again, but this time the sound held no warmth. "Devon has always had a talent for revising history. Did he also tell you about the decades after his 'escape,' when he was every bit the killer I taught him to be? The villages he decimated, the families he destroyed, the humans he kept as playthings until he tired of them?"

Kate maintained her composure, though the words struck at her deepest fears about Devon's past. "He's told me enough. I know he wasn't always the man he is now."

"The man," Elisabeta repeated, amused. "He isn't a man, Katherine. He's a vampire, a predator, a killer. No matter how cultured he seems, that nature remains the same."

"People change," Kate said firmly. "Even vampires."

"Do they?" Elisabeta moved closer, her movements so smooth she seemed to glide across the floor. "Or do they just find more refined ways to give in to their true natures?" Tell me, how did you and Devon meet? Did he approach you openly, honestly? Or did he manipulate circumstances to bring you into his orbit?"

Kate remained silent, unwilling to give Elisabeta the satisfaction of confirming what she clearly already knew: That Devon had arranged their meeting and lured Kate to Budapest with the exhibition opportunity.

"Ah, I see he didn't share that part with you either," Elisabeta said, reading

Kate's expression. "So many secrets between you. So many lies."

"Why are you doing this?" Kate asked, fighting to maintain her mental barriers as Elisabeta's influence pressed against them. "What do you want from me?"

"Want?" Elisabeta seemed genuinely puzzled by the question. "I don't want anything from you, my dear. I'm simply... curious. About what makes you special. About why Devon is willing to risk everything, his standing in vampire society, his very existence, for you."

She circled Kate slowly, examining her from all angles like a sculpture in a museum. "You're beautiful, certainly, but Devon has had beautiful companions before. Your talents are impressive, but he has known greater artists. You're intelligent and spirited, although nothing extraordinary. The words aimed to belittle and make Kate feel small. Even though she knew their intentions, Kate felt the sting of truth in Elisabeta's critique. What was she, really, compared to the immortal beings Devon had known over his centuries of existence?

"And yet," Elisabeta continued, stopping directly in front of Kate, "he loves you. Truly loves you, in a way I didn't think him capable of anymore. It's quite remarkable."

The admission, so at odds with her previous statements, caught Kate off guard. "If you believe that, why try to come between us?"

Elisabeta smiled, revealing the tips of her fangs. "Who says that's my intention? Perhaps I simply want to understand. Perhaps I want to ensure you're worthy of him. Or perhaps..." She leaned closer, her amber eyes seeming to glow in the dim light. "Perhaps I want to offer you a choice."

"What kind of choice?" Kate asked warily.

"A simple one. Leave Devon willingly, disappear from his life completely, and I'll ensure you live a long, prosperous human life. Stay with him, and I'll use you to bring him back to me, where he belongs."

"He doesn't belong to you," Kate said, anger flaring. "He's not your possession."

"Isn't he?" Elisabeta's voice dropped to a hypnotic murmur. "I made him, Katherine. My blood flows in his veins. My power sustains his existence. "In the most basic sense, he is mine and always will be."

Kate felt the pressure against her mental barriers grow stronger. Elisabeta's will pressed against her defences with centuries of force behind it. Images rushed through her mind of Devon when he was newly turned, wild with bloodlust. Devon hunting humans through dark streets; Devon kneeling before Elisabeta in submission.

"Stop it," Kate gasped, pressing her hands to her temples. "Get out of my head."

"These aren't my creations," Elisabeta said gently. "They're his memories, buried deep but never forgotten. This is who he was. Who he still is, beneath the skin."

"No," Kate insisted, though doubt seeped through her like poison. "That's not him anymore."

"Are you certain?" Elisabeta moved even closer, her cool breath fanning Kate's cheek.

"Has he never frightened you? Never made you feel like prey? Never looked at you with hunger that had nothing to do with love?"

Kate couldn't deny it. There had been moments, especially in the beginning, when Devon's vampiric nature had terrified her. When she had seen the monster beneath the man and knew she was completely at his mercy. "He's changed," she repeated, but her voice lacked conviction.

"Has he?" Elisabeta asked again. "Or has he simply found a more willing captive? One who mistakes her cage for a home?"

The words struck at Kate's deepest insecurity, that her love for Devon was some form of Stockholm Syndrome, that she had rationalized her captivity rather than truly choosing him.

"You're wrong," Kate said, but the words sounded hollow even to her own ears.

Elisabeta smiled, sensing victory. "Am I? Then why did you leave him, Katherine? Why are you here alone instead of safely by his side?"

Before Kate could respond, a commotion erupted from the main gallery, raised voices and the sound of breaking glass. Elisabeta's expression shifted from triumph to annoyance. "It seems we have an uninvited guest," she said, moving toward the door. "Excuse me a moment."

Kate slumped against the wall, her mind racing from Elisabeta's psychological attack. The vampire's words had seeped into every part of her confidence about her relationship with Devon. However, beneath that doubt lay anger. She was furious with Elisabeta for trying to ruin what she and Devon had built. She was also angry at herself for letting her words affect her so much.

Kate straightened, reinforcing her mental shields. Whatever game Elisabeta was playing, Kate refused to be toyed with. The door burst open, and Devon stood there, his normally composed features twisted with a mixture of fear and rage Kate had never seen before.

"Kate," Devon said, his voice rough with emotion. "Are you hurt?"

"No," she said, moving toward him. "I'm okay."

Relief flooded his face, quickly replaced by determination. "We need to leave. Now."

"Not so fast, my darling," Elisabeta's voice came from behind him. "We haven't finished our conversation."

Devon turned, positioning himself between Kate and his maker. "Stay away from her, Elisabeta."

Elisabeta laughed, the sound genuinely amused. "Or what? What will you do, my creation? Fight me? We both know how that would end."

Before Devon could react, Elisabeta's hand shot out with inhuman speed, grasping his wrist. There was a sickening crack, and Devon's face contorted in pain as she twisted his arm at an impossible angle, snapping the bones like twigs, before dropping his hand without a second thought.

Kate looked on in horror as Devon's wrist began to heal right in front of her eyes, the bones knitting back together at a rapid speed. From the main gallery came the sound of breaking glass and a cry of pain.

"Your friend is putting up quite a fight," Elisabeta said conversationally. "But Nikolai and Siobhan are very experienced. I do hope he doesn't get himself killed on your behalf."

Devon's jaw tightened. "Call them off."

"Why would I do that? This is all quite entertaining." Elisabeta moved to the window, pulling back the heavy curtain to peer out at the street. "Though I suppose we should wrap this up soon. The neighbors might start to complain about the noise."

Kate had never seen Devon afraid, truly afraid, until this moment. He stood rigid with tension, his body practically vibrating with it, yet she could see the terror beneath his defiance.

"I won't let you hurt her," Devon said, his voice steadier than his posture.

"Hurt her?" Elisabeta seemed offended by the suggestion. "I've done nothing of the sort. We were simply having a civilized conversation about you, weren't we, Katherine?"

Kate moved to stand beside Devon rather than behind him. "You call psychological manipulation civilized?"

Elisabeta's eyes widened slightly, the first genuine surprise Kate had seen from her. "Interesting. Your mental shields are stronger than I expected. Devon has taught you well."

"Enough," Devon repeated, his wrist finally healed enough for him to clench his hands at his sides. "Your quarrel is with me, not her."

"Quarrel?" Elisabeta shook her head. "Oh, Devon. Always so dramatic. I have no quarrel with either of you. I was simply satisfying my curiosity about the human who has captured your heart so completely."

"And now that your curiosity is satisfied?" Devon asked warily.

Elisabeta studied Kate with renewed interest. "Not entirely. But I've learned enough for one evening." She stepped aside, gesturing toward the door. "You may go. Both of you."

Devon hesitated, clearly suspecting a trap. "Just like that?"

"Just like that," Elisabeta confirmed. "For now."

The implicit threat hung in the air between them. This wasn't over; it was simply postponed. Devon took Kate's hand, his grip almost painfully tight.

"Come on," he murmured. "Before she changes her mind."

They moved past Elisabeta, who watched them with eyes that seemed ancient and unreadable. At the threshold, she called out, "Katherine."

Kate paused, looking back despite Devon's attempt to pull her forward.

"Remember what I said," Elisabeta told her. "About choices. About cages. About who he really is."

"I know who he is," Kate replied steadily. "Better than you ever did."

Before she could respond, Devon pulled Kate through the door and into the main gallery. The scene that greeted them was one of controlled chaos. Furniture lay overturned and broken, artwork hung askew on the walls or lay shattered on the floor. Antoine stood near the entrance, holding off three vampires with nothing but his presence and what Kate assumed was considerable age and power. Antoine's usually immaculate suit was torn and bloodied, his face bearing the marks of a vicious fight. The other gallery "attendees" had vanished, fled or hidden, Kate couldn't tell.

"Time to go," Antoine said tersely as they approached. "My car is outside."

They moved as a unit toward the exit, Devon keeping Kate between himself and Antoine. No one tried to stop them, on Elisabeta's orders, Kate presumed. Outside, a sleek black car idled at the curb. Antoine opened the rear door, and Devon ushered Kate inside before sliding in beside her. Antoine took the driver's seat, and they pulled away from the curb with controlled urgency.

"Are you really alright?" Devon asked once they were moving, his hands checking her for injuries with gentle insistence.

"I'm fine," Kate assured him, though 'fine' was far from accurate. She was physically unharmed but mentally and emotionally shaken; Elisabeta's words still echoed in her head. "But what about you? Elisabeta broke your wrist."

Devon let out a hoarse laugh, the sound strained and disbelieving. "You're worried about me? Kate, I'm a vampire. It healed completely before we even left the building." He demonstrated by flexing his fingers. "But thank you for your concern."

"We heal quite quickly," Antoine added from the front seat, his voice warm with reassurance. "A few cuts and bruises are nothing. We'll both be good as new by morning."

"What did she say to you?" Devon asked, his voice tight with concern.

Kate hesitated, unsure how to sum up the conversation between Elisabeta and herself. "She tried to make me doubt you. Us. Everything."

Devon's face darkened. "Whatever she told you—"

"Can we talk about it later?" Kate interrupted, suddenly aware of their audience. Antoine might be Devon's friend, but he was still a vampire, still a stranger to her.

Devon nodded, understanding her reluctance. "Of course."

They rode in silence for several minutes, the city passing in a blur outside the windows. Kate soon realized that they weren't heading toward Zoe's apartment or the penthouse in Tribeca.

"Where are we going?" she asked.

"Somewhere safe," Antoine answered from the front seat. "A property I maintain for emergencies. Elisabeta doesn't know about it."

Kate wanted to object, insist on returning to Zoe's, but she was exhausted. The adrenaline that had kept her going through the confrontation was fading, leaving her drained and shaky.

"I need to let Zoe know I'm okay," she said instead. "She'll worry."

Devon handed her his phone. "The signal is secure."

Kate sent a quick text to Zoe, explaining that she was safe but staying with friends tonight. It wasn't the whole truth, but it would prevent Zoe from calling the police when Kate didn't return.

As she handed the phone back, her fingers brushed against Devon's, and she saw that his hands were trembling slightly. Kate looked at him for the first time since they had escaped and noticed how shaken he appeared. The calm, composed vampire she once knew was gone, replaced by someone who seemed noticeably uneasy. His eyes showed fears she could hardly grasp. Without thinking, Kate took his hand and intertwined her fingers with his. Devon looked at their joined hands with surprise, then at her face, a question in his eyes.

"I'm still angry," Kate said softly. "About the lies. About all of it. But I'm glad you came for me tonight."

Devon's expression softened, relief and gratitude replacing some of the fear. "I will always come for you, Kate. Always."

The simple declaration, spoken with such certainty, cut through some of the doubt Elisabeta had planted. Whatever else was true or false between them, Kate believed that Devon would move heaven and earth to protect her, not because she was his possession, but because she was his everything.

As the car carried them through the night toward an unknown sanctuary,

Kate leaned against Devon's shoulder, allowing herself this moment of connection despite the unresolved issues between them. They had survived Elisabeta's ambush, but Kate somehow knew that it was only the beginning.

The ancient vampire had set her sights on them both, and she had eternity to play her games. The only question was whether their bond would strengthen under the pressure or crumble completely.

Chapter 15

Antoine drove them to an apartment in a unremarkable building in Midtown, one that blended in with the surrounding skyscrapers. Inside, however, it was a fortress of elegant luxury with reinforced windows and a state-of-the-art security system. A quiet sanctuary.

"You'll be safe here," Antoine assured them, his gaze lingering on Kate with a mixture of concern and curiosity. "Elisabeta doesn't know about this location. Few do."

Kate sank onto a plush velvet sofa, her body trembling with exhaustion. The adrenaline that had carried her through the confrontation at the gallery had long since faded, leaving her feeling raw and exposed. Devon hovered nearby, his anxiety a tangible presence in the room.

"Thank you, Antoine," Devon said, his voice still rough with emotion. "I am in your debt."

"Consider it partial repayment for Prague," Antoine replied with a faint smile. "A word before I leave?"

The two vampires stepped onto the terrace, their voices low and indistinct as they discussed security measures. Kate leaned her head back against the sofa, closing her eyes. She could feel Devon's gaze on her even from the terrace, his worry like a physical weight. When Antoine finally departed, Devon returned to the living room, his expression still tight with concern. He sat beside Kate, leaving a careful distance between them.

"Tell me more about vampire law," Kate said, breaking the silence. "About makers and their progeny. You mentioned before that killing your maker is... taboo."

Devon's hand moved unconsciously to his throat, and his eyes grew distant, unfocused.

"Devon?" Kate prompted gently.

He blinked, returning to the present. With deliberate slowness, he unbuttoned the top two buttons of his shirt and pulled the collar to reveal the silvery-white scar she had noticed at the Met a few days prior. It was an intricate pattern that resembled a brand or scar, but with an unnatural sheen that seemed to catch the light differently than the surrounding skin.

"This is the physical manifestation of the maker bond," Devon said, his voice low. "Every vampire carries one."

Kate leaned closer, fascinated despite herself. The mark was beautiful in its way, an elaborate design that resembled a stylized knot or sigil, about the size of a silver dollar.

"May I?" she asked, her hand hovering near his neck.

Devon nodded, though she noticed a slight tension in his jaw. As Kate traced the pattern, Devon's eyes fluttered closed, his breathing changing subtly. The mark felt cooler than the rest of his skin, with a texture that was somehow both smooth and electric.

"It's a channel," he continued, rebuttoning his shirt. "A connection that binds maker and progeny across time and distance."

As if to demonstrate, Devon closed his eyes. The lights in the apartment flickered briefly, and Kate felt a sudden chill in the air. When Devon opened his eyes again, they had darkened unnaturally.

"Even now, centuries later, if she focuses her will…" His voice trailed off as his hand clenched involuntarily into a fist. "I can feel her. Like phantom pain from a wound that never fully healed."

Kate watched as Devon visibly struggled against something she couldn't see. After a moment, he exhaled slowly, and his body relaxed.

"The bond is considered sacred in vampire society," he said. "To sever it through violence is to invite condemnation from the entire vampire world. The Council would hunt me down. I'd be an outcast, a pariah."

"So we're trapped," Kate said, despair creeping into her voice.

"Not entirely," Devon said, moving closer, his hand covering hers. "Elisabeta could release me willingly, but it's something she has refused to do for four centuries."

Kate looked at their joined hands, processing this information. "We'll find a way," she said, though she wasn't sure she believed it.

Devon squeezed her hand, his thumb tracing circles on her skin. The mark at his throat had settled again, returning to its silvery stillness.

"We will," he said softly. "Together."

"Devon," she began, her voice trembling slightly. "Elisabeta… she said things. About your past. About the things you did after you escaped her. She told me you were a predator. That you destroyed villages, kept humans as playthings. Is it true?"

Devon looked away, his profile outlined in shadow against the city lights. When he finally spoke, his voice was filled with regret. "Yes," he said simply. "It's true."

Kate felt a cold knot form in her stomach. "Why didn't you tell me?"

"Shame," Devon whispered, turning back to her, his eyes full of deep pain. "Because that part of me, the monster I became in those first decades of freedom, is something I've spent centuries trying to forget. To atone for."

"I understand shame, Devon," Kate said softly. "But I don't understand secrets. Not anymore. Not between us."

Devon nodded, his gaze focused on their joined hands. "After I escaped Elisabeta, I was filled with bloodlust. For years, I hunted indiscriminately. I was everything she had made me, a monster." He paused, struggling. "It took decades for the madness to fade. Decades of violence and regret before I began to find my way back to some semblance of humanity."

Kate listened in silence, her heart aching for the fledgling vampire Devon had once been.

"I'm not proud of who I was in those early years," Devon whispered. "But it's a part of me that I can't deny, no matter how much I might want to."

Kate reached out and traced the line of his jaw with her fingers. "Thank you for trusting me with this."

Devon leaned into her touch, briefly closing his eyes. "I should have told you sooner. I should have trusted you from the beginning."

"We both made mistakes," Kate admitted. "But we can learn from them. We can choose to be honest with each other, even when it's hard."

Devon opened his eyes, his gaze searching hers. "Can you forgive me, Kate? For the lies?"

"I already have," she whispered, and knew in that moment it was true. Her anger had faded, replaced by a deeper understanding of the man beside her, his flaws, his fears, his centuries of pain. And with that forgiveness came something else, a wave of emotion so powerful it stole her breath. Love, yes, but also desire, a desperate need to bridge their division and renew their connection.

She leaned forward to find his lips in a kiss that was both timid and urgent. Devon didn't hold back; his arms wrapped around her and drew her close until they had no distance left between them. It was a kiss of forgiveness, of acceptance, and a love that had been tested and found stronger.

Devon's control began to fray despite his centuries of discipline. His hands roamed her body, no longer possessive but predatory, mapping the curves of her breasts, the swell of her hips, squeezing with a force that made her gasp. Kate arched against him, a low moan rumbling in her chest, her fingers clawing at his hair, pulling him closer. She wanted to be devoured.

His mouth left hers to trail down her neck, his tongue a hot brand against her skin. His fangs brushed her pulse, sending a thrilling shiver down her spine. "I've missed the taste of you," he rasped, sliding his hands under her shirt. He lifted her as if she weighed nothing and pressed her against the wall.

Their clothes became an intolerable barrier, torn away in a frenzy of urgent hands and teeth. When he knelt down to remove her panties, he didn't bother pulling them down. She felt the shocking, thrilling scrape of his fangs as he bit into the fabric, tearing it away from her body with a sharp rip. He spat the ruined silk to the floor, his eyes meeting hers with dark satisfaction, and then his mouth was on her.

He devoured her, his tongue a relentless, masterful instrument. The first stroke against her gleaming core made her scream his name. Her fingers dug into his shoulders. He was a predator savoring his prey, and Kate writhed beneath him, coherent thought dissolving under the onslaught of sensation. His hands gripped her hips, pinning her to the wall as he lapped and sucked with an unyielding rhythm. Her world melted into a blur of sensation, from the exquisite friction, the cool wall against her back, to the hot, wet magic of his skilled mouth. He brought her to the edge, held her there until she was begging, and then with a final, expert flick, sent her crashing over. Her orgasm was a violent, shuddering wave, a ragged cry torn from her throat as he drank down her release.

Before the last tremor had faded, he was moving up her body, his lips slick, his eyes blazing with triumph. He lifted Kate, wrapping her legs around his waist and pinning her once again to the wall. The hard length of him pressed hot and demanding against her entrance. She reached between them, her hand wrapping around his cock, guiding him to where she needed him most. He pushed forward in a single, brutal thrust that filled her completely, tearing a gasp from both of them.

"Mine," Devon growled, the word vibrating through her as he began to move. "My Kate."

"Always," she sobbed, hooking her legs around his waist, pulling him deeper.

Their rhythm was frantic, a desperate, greedy claiming. He possessed her body and soul, right there against the wall, the slap of their bodies echoing through the apartment. She could feel the tension coiling inside her again, impossibly soon, impossibly intense.

"Turn around", he commanded, his voice rough with desire that bordered on madness. He pulled out, and she nearly cried at the loss, but he spun her around, pressing her hands flat against the wall. He entered her from behind, one hand gripping her hip, the other tangling in her hair, pulling her head back. The new angle was devastating. He set a relentless pace, and just as she felt her legs begin to quiver, his hand slid down from her hair to wrap around her throat in a possessive gesture that made her breath catch. The vulnerability of the position and the trust it required sent a fresh wave of heat through her.

"Come for me, Kate," he commanded against her ear, his voice strained with his own approaching release.

The combination was too much. Her second orgasm ripped through her, even more intense than the first, her entire body trembling with the force of it. He followed a moment later, his own release a guttural groan, her name a reverent cry on his lips as he emptied himself inside her.

They stayed like that for a long moment, both panting, his forehead pressed against the back of her neck, his arms wrapped around her waist to keep her upright. When he finally pulled out, she felt the warm rush of their combined pleasure trail down her inner thigh, a tangible reminder of the passion they'd just shared.

Devon turned her gently, his hands suddenly tender as he cupped her face. "Are you alright?" he asked, his eyes searching hers with concern that cut through the haze of pleasure.

"More than alright," she whispered, her voice hoarse. Her legs were shaking, and he seemed to notice, because he scooped her up and carried her to the bedroom, laying her gently on the cool sheets.

He disappeared into the bathroom and returned with a warm, damp cloth. Kate watched him through heavy-lidded eyes as he knelt between her thighs, cleaning her with a care that was achingly tender. When he was done, he tossed the cloth aside and stretched out beside her, pulling her into his arms.

They lay entangled, their breathing slowly returning to normal. Kate traced slow patterns on his chest, her fingers following the defined lines of muscle. She felt the pleasant ache in her muscles and the tender spots where his fingers had gripped her hips. It reminded her that this was real, that he was here, and that they had found their way back to each other.

"I love you," she whispered, the words carrying a certainty that resonated deep in her soul.

Devon pulled her closer, his lips brushing her forehead, then her temple, then finding her mouth in a soft kiss. "I love you too, Katherine Morgan," he murmured against her lips. "More than I have words to express. More than I thought possible after all these centuries."

They lay in post-coital silence for a long time, the city lights painting shadows across their skin. When dawn neared, Devon stirred and his arms tightened around her. "I should go," he murmured. "Stay, just a little longer,"

Kate whispered, kissing his shoulder. He held her until the first rays of sunlight touched the horizon. He pressed one last kiss to her lips and then reluctantly pulled away.

The lies and secrets were gone, replaced by honesty and renewed trust. They were a team again, united against a common enemy, ready to shape their future.

Chapter 16

The day following their reconciliation was a fragile truce with the world. The raw honesty of Devon's confessions had forged a new, stronger intimacy between them, but the threat of Elisabeta still loomed, a shadow at the edge of their sanctuary.

Kate found herself pacing the length of Antoine's luxurious, sterile apartment. She was not a prisoner here, she told herself, trying to make the words feel true. She was a guest. A protected asset. But the reinforced windows and the knowledge that she couldn't leave felt all too familiar.

She walked to the giant window and looked out at the city below. People were rushing to work, grabbing coffee, living their simple, sunlit lives. A wave of deep longing washed over her. She saw her own reflection in the glass, a pale and tired woman. For a heart-stopping moment, she wondered what that other life would have looked like. A life with a human partner, children, a life of brunch dates and shared holidays, of growing old together.

Was the epic, all-consuming love she felt for Devon worth this? Fear, gilded cages, goodbye to the world she could no longer be a part of?

When dusk arrived in Manhattan, Devon rose with a cold, clear purpose. His vulnerability from the previous night has vanished, locked away behind a mask of calculating efficiency. He found Kate in the living area, her sketchbook open on the coffee table, the scent of charcoal in the air.

"Antoine will be here soon", he said, his voice low and controlled. "He's been making inquiries through his network."

Kate closed the sketchbook, the action feeling like a deliberate closing of a door on her doubts. "And what will you be doing?"

"Contacting my own allies," he replied. "Those loyal to me, not just to the old ways. We need to understand her movements, her resources in this city."

When Antoine arrived, the two vampires spoke in low tones, sometimes in English, sometimes in other, older languages that Kate didn't recognize. Names were mentioned like chess pieces, allies, enemies, neutral parties. Maps of the city were displayed on a tablet. Surveillance images of Elisabeta's New York townhouse were splayed across the table. Financial transactions were traced. It was a glimpse into a world of ancient politics and hidden power that operated just beneath the surface of her own.

Devon was a different person. He was the otherworldly creature she had first met, but his focus was not on her. It was a cold, ruthless intelligence directed outward, a formidable force now bent entirely on her protection. He was terrifying, and she had never loved him more.

Late into the night, Antoine reentered the room after taking a phone call, his expression more serious than usual.

"We have a problem," he said without small talk. "My source at Teterboro Airport has confirmed it. A private jet, chartered under one of Elisabeta's known corporate identities, filed a flight plan one hour ago."

Devon went still, his focus absolute. "Destination?"

"Le Bourget," Antoine replied. "Paris."

The name hung in the air, cold and heavy with implication.

"Paris," Devon breathed, understanding immediately. "The Vampire Council. She's not just making a move against us; she's making a move against me on the world stage. She's taking this to the highest authority." His eyes met Antoine's, a silent question passing between them.

As if in answer, Antoine's phone chimed. He read the message, and his face hardened.

"We're too late to stop it," he said, his voice flat. "My source at the Council just confirmed it. A petition has been accepted. The Council has issued a formal summons. You are to appear before them. In three nights."

Chapter 17

The silence that followed Antoine's departure was heavier and colder than any they had shared before. The news of the Council summons had sucked the air from the room, leaving a vacuum filled with unspoken dread. Paris. In three nights. It was no longer a threat; it was a death sentence on a timetable.

Kate watched Devon as he stood by the window, his back to her, gazing out at the city lights. He was unnaturally still, but she could feel the storm raging within him, a tempest of fury, shame, and a fear so ingrained it seemed to make the shadows in the room deepen.

"You don't understand," he said finally, his voice so low it was almost a whisper. "You think this is a debate. A political hearing. You think you can face them with logic and courage, and that will be enough."

"It has to be," Kate said, her own voice a fragile thread of defiance. "It's all we have."

"No," he said, turning to face her. The look in his eyes was one she had never seen before, not the lover, not the protector, not even the captor. It was the look of an ancient being stripped of all pretense, a look of raw, terrifying pity. "It's not all we have. It's all you have. And it is not enough."

He took a step toward her, his movements slow and deliberate. "You know of our speed, our strength. You've seen it. But you haven't felt it. Not really. You don't understand the sheer scale of the power you are so willing to walk amongst."

"I'm not afraid of you, Devon."

"You should be," he whispered, and his eyes changed. The warmth vanished, the pupils dilating until they were black pits of pure predator. His voice dropped, taking on a strange, hypnotic resonance that vibrated in the air, in her very bones. "Sit down, Kate."

It wasn't a request. It was a command woven into sound. Her body reacted before her mind could. Her legs buckled, and she sank onto the edge of the sofa, the movement clumsy, involuntary. A wave of nausea and vertigo washed over her. She had not chosen to sit. Her body had simply obeyed the sound of his voice.'

"What did you do?" she gasped, her hands gripping the velvet cushion, her own muscles suddenly feeling like foreign objects.

"Compulsion," he said, his voice still holding that terrifying, melodic quality. He remained by the window, his distance making the violation even more unsettling. He wasn't even touching her. "A whisper of will. A tool for controlling prey. For making humans… compliant. Elisabeta has had eight centuries to perfect it. I have spent almost as long learning to suppress it." He took another step closer. "Take off your necklace."

Her hands flew to her throat, her fingers fumbling with the clasp of the silver pendant he had given her. *No, her mind screamed. Don't do it. It's a trick. Fight it.* But her fingers wouldn't obey. They worked at the delicate chain with a frantic, desperate purpose that was not her own. The silver felt cold against her skin. With a soft click, the clasp came undone. She was holding the pendant in her palm, her hand trembling.

Tears of pure, violated rage welled in her eyes. This was what he had been hiding. This was the power he had been "curbing." It wasn't just strength or speed. It was the power to erase her, to turn her into a puppet.

Before she could react, he moved. It wasn't the fluid grace she was used to. This was a violation of physics. One instant he was across the room, the next he was directly in front of her, his hand clasped around her throat. There was no sound, no rush of air. He had simply ceased to be there and begun to be here.

His grip was not tight. It was a feather-light touch, his cool fingers resting on her pulse. But the implication was clear. He could snap her neck before her brain could even register his touch. Kate's breath hitched, her body frozen, not by compulsion, but by a primal, animal fear. This was not Devon. This was something else.

"This is what they are," he whispered, his voice now a sibilant, inhuman sound that seemed to come from the air around them. "This is the speed with which they can kill you. This is how little your strength, your courage, your will, matters to them."

He released her, and in the same impossible instant, he was across the room, holding one of the heavy, solid-wood chairs from the dining set. He held it aloft with one hand as if it were made of paper.

"Their strength," he said. He squeezed his hand, and the chair didn't just break; it imploded. Wood shattered into a thousand pieces, joints exploding outward with a sound like a cannon blast. The destruction was so total, so effortless, it defied reason.

He was by her side again, his hand now gently tracing the line of her jaw, his touch a terrifying counterpoint to the violence she had just witnessed. He opened his hand, and her necklace was resting in his palm. He had taken it from her grasp without her even perceiving the movement. He opened his eyes, and they were Devon's again, filled with an anguish that made her want to hold him. The monster was gone, and her partner was back, his face a mask of shame.

"That," he said, his voice ragged and human once more, "is what you are facing. That is Elisabeta. That is Viktor. That is what I have been trying, and failing, to protect you from."

Kate's body trembled as she sat frozen, her mind recovering from the violation she had just experienced. Now she finally understood. Just because she hadn't witnessed the violence of vampires firsthand did not mean it didn't exist. His fear, his suffocating need for control, it wasn't about possessing her. It was about trying to protect a fragile, slow, human thing from the casual wrath of gods.

They were not just partners in love. They were partners in a war she was only now beginning to understand. But something else burned away too, her fear. Not the healthy caution that would keep her alive, but the paralyzing terror that had gripped her when his hand closed around her throat. What remained was something far more dangerous: A reckless, desperate hunger. Kate stood up, her heart hammering with a desperate, defiant energy. Her voice, when she spoke, was tight with challenge.

"You've been holding back," she stated, her eyes locked on his. "All this time, you've been treating me like I'm made of glass. For my sake."

Devon's jaw clenched, a muscle twitching in his cheek. "Kate, don't."

"Don't what?" she shot back, her fingers moving to the buttons of her blouse. It wasn't a seduction; it was a dare. "Don't ask for the real you? I want to see all of you, Devon. I need to know that you aren't holding a part of yourself back from me." The first button slipped free, then the second. "I need to know I can handle it."

"No." The word was torn from him, raw and desperate. His hands shot out, not to touch her, but as if to ward her off. "You don't understand what you're asking."

But Kate was fueled by a frantic need to prove him wrong. To prove to herself that the relationship she'd staked her life on was real. She pulled away from his unspoken plea and let her blouse fall to the floor, her movements sharp and challenging.

"I understand perfectly," she said, her voice trembling slightly. "I understand that you see me as fragile. That you believe the very essence of what you are is too much for me."

Devon's control was visibly fracturing. She could see it in the rigid set of his shoulders, in the way his eyes had gone completely black.

"Kate, stop." His voice was a low growl, barely human. "This isn't a game. If I don't hold back, if I let go completely… I could rip you in two."

The words weren't arousing. They were a bucket of ice water, extinguishing the fire of her defiance and leaving a cold, sickening dread in its place. It was then she realized that he wasn't just being careful; he was managing a lethal threat. Her.

All this time, she'd been telling herself they were equals. She had built her entire sense of self around the idea that she was no longer his captive, but his partner. It had been a beautiful, dangerous delusion. Standing there, half-naked and trembling, she finally understood the truth. They weren't equals. They never could be. She was a fragile, breakable thing that he had to constantly protect, even from himself.

"I'm not your equal," she whispered, the words tasting bitter on her tongue. "I never was, was I?"

Devon's face crumpled, pain flashing in his eyes. "Kate, no. You are my equal in every way that matters—"

"How could I be?" she challenged, her voice breaking as she wrapped her arms around herself. "Can I protect you? Can I match your strength? Can I even survive your touch without you having to think about it?" She took a shaky step back. "That's not a partnership, Devon. That's… that's you taking care of a Pet."

The word hung between them like a guillotine. Devon flinched as if she'd struck him.

"Don't," he whispered, his voice ragged. "You are not that. You have never been that."

But the damage was done. The word, Pet, echoed in the space between them, and Kate became acutely aware of her state of undress. Heat flooded her cheeks, not from desire, but from a deep, burning shame.

She had tried to prove she was a lioness, only to be told, in no uncertain terms, that she was a lamb he was kind enough not to devour.

Her hands flew to cover herself as she scrambled for her discarded blouse. "I need to—" she started, her voice thick with humiliation.

"Kate, please—" Devon stepped toward her, his own pain a tangible force in the room.

She backed away. "Don't," she echoed, her voice cracking. "Just… don't."

She grabbed her blouse, her movements jerky and desperate. The silk felt foreign as she struggled with buttons that seemed impossibly small. Now she felt like a child playing dress-up in adult clothes, pretending to be something she simply wasn't. Devon stood frozen, watching her retreat.

"Kate, what we have, it's not what you said."

"Isn't it?" She finally managed to get the blouse on, though it hung open. "Look at me, Devon. I'm standing here, shaking, because you told me the truth. That you could kill me without thinking." Tears she hadn't realized were building spilled over. "I thought I was strong. I thought we were… equals." She let out a broken, humorless laugh. "God, I was so naive."

"You are strong," Devon insisted, his voice laced with anguish. "The fact that you demanded this, that you weren't afraid—"

"I'm not afraid of you," Kate interrupted, wiping at her eyes. "I'm afraid of what I am to you. A fragile human who's been playing pretend." She finally looked at him, her gaze clear and cold. "How can I have truly chosen this life, chosen you, if I never even understood the terms?"

The silence that followed was deafening.

"I need a moment," she whispered, finally managing to button her blouse. "I need to… process."

She moved toward the bedroom, but his voice stopped her.

"Kate." It was soft, broken. "Please don't run from me."

She turned back, the pain in his ancient eyes nearly undoing her. "I'm not running," she said quietly. "I'm just… seeing things clearly for the first time. And I need to understand what it means."

"It means you are my heart, my soul, my reason for being," he said fiercely, closing the distance between them but stopping just short of touching her. "You are not my Pet, Kate. You are my choice. You don't need to be anything other than who you are. What you are is perfect."

Kate leaned into his touch. "What I am is human. And you…" She looked up at him. "You've been denying a fundamental part of yourself to keep me safe."

"When I'm with you, I feel more human than I have in centuries," he said urgently.

"But you're not human," Kate said softly. "And I think I've been asking you to be."

They stood there, the comfortable illusions they'd built around their relationship shattered on the floor.

"So where does that leave us?" Kate asked.

Devon's thumb traced her cheekbone. "I don't know," he admitted. "But I know I can't lose you. I won't survive it."

"You won't lose me," Kate promised. "But we need to build this on truth.

Not on what we wish we were, but on what we actually are."

Devon nodded slowly. "And what is that?"

Kate considered it, looking at this ancient, powerful being who loved her. "I think," she said carefully, "you're someone who chose to love a fragile, human woman, knowing the cost. And I'm the woman who chose to love an immortal."

"Is that enough for you?" Devon asked, his voice soft.

Kate thought about the future, the Council, and the dangers circling them. The fear was still there, but now it was grounded in reality, not fantasy.

"Ask me again in Paris," she said. "After we see if we can survive what's coming."

He nodded, understanding. "And until then?"

Kate stepped into his arms, resting her forehead against his chest. "Until then, we learn how to be what we are."

He held her, his embrace careful and protective. "I can live with that," he murmured.

"Good," Kate said, closing her eyes. "Because it's the only honest thing we've got."

Chapter 18

The morning following Devon's terrifying demonstration felt different. As he settled into his daylight sleep, Kate was left alone with the lingering fear and aching loneliness of her new reality. She looked at the vampire sleeping in the bed, the creature who had erased her will with a whisper and shattered a chair with a thought, and felt an overwhelming urge for the one thing he could never truly give her: The simple, uncomplicated comfort of her mother. She picked up her phone, her hands still trembling slightly.

"Katie? Is everything alright?" Eleanor Morgan answered on the first ring, her voice sharp with a mother's intuition.

"Everything's fine, Mom," Kate lied, the words tasting like ash. "I… I was just wondering if you were free today. For lunch, maybe? Or just tea?"

There was a pause on the other end of the line. "Of course, sweetheart. Anything for you. Where are you?"

A few hours later, Kate was sitting in the familiar, sun-drenched kitchen of her childhood home. The sight of her mother moving with practiced ease through the space was all so painfully normal it felt like a scene from another life. A mortal life.

"You look like you haven't slept in a week," Eleanor said, placing a steaming mug in front of her, her gaze gentle but missing nothing.

"It's been a lot," Kate admitted, wrapping her hands around the mug's warmth. The simple pleasure of hot coffee, the way it warmed her human body, would she miss these small comforts if she chose Devon's path?

They sat in silence for a few moments before Eleanor spoke again. "Your father and I… we're worried, Katie. This whirlwind romance, this man who seems to have appeared out of nowhere… he's charming, I'll give him that. But there's a sadness in him. And now he's whisking you away to Paris with no warning. We don't understand."

"I know," Kate said, her voice thick with emotion. "And I'm sorry I can't explain it better. It's…complicated."

"All love is complicated," Eleanor said softly. "But this feels different. When you look at him, there's so much love in your eyes, but there's something else too. Like you're standing at the edge of a cliff, deciding whether to jump."

The metaphor was more on point than her mother could have known. Kate felt tears prick her eyes.

"Mom, what would you do if you loved someone so much that you'd be willing to change everything about your life for them? Even if it meant… even if it meant leaving your old life behind completely?"

Eleanor's expression grew serious, her maternal instincts clearly sensing the weight behind the question.

"That's a big question, sweetheart. Are we talking about moving to Europe? Changing careers?"

"Something like that," Kate said carefully. "Something that would mean I could never really come back to this life. This version of myself."

Eleanor reached across the table and took her daughter's hand, her grip firm and steady. "Katie, I've watched you your whole life. You've always been drawn to intensity, to experiences that transform you. Your art, your passions, you don't do anything halfway." She paused, studying Kate's face. "The question isn't whether you'd be willing to change for love. The question is whether that change would make you more yourself, or less."

Kate felt her breath catch. "What do you mean?"

"I mean, would this change, whatever it is, allow you to be the fullest version of who you are? Or would you need to edit yourself? Because real love doesn't ask you to become smaller, Katie. It lets you become more."

The words hit Kate like a revelation. She thought about her relationship with Devon, about how he'd encouraged her art, pushed her to be stronger and braver than she'd ever imagined. Even his protection of her came from a place of wanting to preserve who she was, not control her.

"He makes me feel like I could be anything," Kate whispered. "Like I could be... more than I ever thought possible."

Eleanor smiled, a knowing expression that spoke of decades of marriage and motherhood. "Then maybe the question isn't whether you should change for him. Maybe it's whether you're brave enough to become who you're meant to be."

They spent the rest of the day together, but Kate found herself seeing everything through new eyes. Her mother's garden, where she'd played as a child, would she miss the simple pleasure of sunlight on her skin? The photo albums filled with family memories, would she still be able to be part of this world if she chose immortality?

As the day wore on, Kate realized she wasn't mourning the loss of her human life, but celebrating what it had given her: The strength, love, and artistic vision that had brought her to this moment. If she chose transformation, she wouldn't be losing herself. She'd be taking everything she was and making it eternal. When dusk began to fall, she knew she had to leave. Eleanor hugged her fiercely at the door.

"Whatever you're facing, you face it together," she whispered. "That's what a partnership is. And Katie? Whatever choice you make, make it with your whole heart. Don't look back."

Kate laughed, a real laugh that broke through the tension. "I love you, Mom."

"I love you too, sweetheart. Now go. That mysterious European of yours is probably wondering where you've disappeared to all day."

Kate felt tears prick her eyes. "Thank you for understanding, Mom. Even when I can't explain everything."

"I don't need to know the details," Eleanor said gently. "But I know you, Kate. And I know that whatever choice you're facing, you'll make the right one. Trust yourself."

Kate felt a sudden sense of clarity. Her mother was right, this wasn't about changing for Devon. She was choosing to become the fullest version of herself. If that version happened to be a vampire, well, perhaps that was simply what she was meant to be.

Chapter 19

Driving away from her childhood home in Montclair towards the city, Kate realized that the quiet, meaningful conversation with her mother had settled the resolve in her heart. Now, there was one last anchor to her human life she had to touch before they stepped into the abyss of Paris. She needed to see Zoe.

Devon, understanding her need to ground herself, had agreed without argument. He seemed to know that these connections were not a distraction, but the very source of the strength she would need to draw upon. Their last stop before heading to the airport was a familiar, paint-scented loft in Bushwick. The light was on, a beacon in the dark.

Zoe opened the door, her arms crossed, her expression a carefully constructed mask of irritation over a sea of deep concern.

"A midnight farewell? Really? You know, for a guy who's supposed to be your partner, he's got you acting like you're in a spy movie."

"It's complicated, Zo," Kate said, stepping into the familiar, beloved chaos of the apartment.

"It's always complicated with you two," Zoe retorted, but her voice softened as she truly looked at Kate's face, her artist's eye catching the faint tremors of exhaustion, the new, hard-won steel in her gaze. "Are you okay? For real."

"I'm okay," Kate lied, "I will be. We're going to Paris to… sort things out. With his family." The euphemism felt flimsy, absurd.

Zoe's gaze shifted to Devon, who had remained quietly by the door, a silent, imposing guardian giving them their space. Her eyes narrowed. "This 'sorting out,'" she said, her voice sharp and low, "it's not going to hurt her, is it? Because she's been through enough."

"Zoe," Kate said, a warning in her tone.

"No, she's right to ask," Devon said, stepping forward. He met Zoe's glare without flinching, his expression one of solemn sincerity. There was no aristocratic charm now, only raw honesty.

"I broke her trust. Badly. And I will spend the rest of my existence earning it back. Everything we are doing now is to ensure her safety and her future."

Zoe studied him for a long, hard moment, searching for any hint of deception. She saw no lies, but she saw a depth of danger and sorrow that made her shiver. Finally, she sighed, her shoulders slumping as she turned back to Kate, her eyes full of a fierce, unwavering love.

"I don't get it. I don't get you," she said, gesturing vaguely at Devon. "But I get her." She took Kate's hands, her grip tight. "You're my family, Kate. You're my person. If you say you trust him, then I'll try. But if he messes up again, you call me. I don't care what continent you're on. I will fly there myself, and I will kick his aristocratic ass."

Kate laughed, a real, watery laugh that broke through the tension. "I'll hold you to that." She pulled her friend into a hug, breathing in the familiar scent of turpentine and friendship, a scent of home.

"I love you, Zoe."

"Just come back," Zoe whispered into her hair, her voice thick with emotion. "Okay? Just… come back."

"I will," Kate promised, a promise she desperately hoped she could keep.

They hugged then, fierce and desperate, two friends who had shared everything now facing the possibility of a separation that might be permanent. When they pulled apart, both had tears in their eyes.

Zoe turned to Devon, her expression serious. "Take care of her," she said simply.

Devon stepped forward, his expression solemn. "With my life," he said, and Kate knew he meant it literally.

Kate and Devon stepped out into the cool New York night, Kate feeling the weight of her two worlds. She had said her goodbyes, shoring up the human connections that grounded her, the promises that defined her.

Now, it was time to face the immortal ones and make her choice.

Chapter 20

The private jet cut through the night sky, its luxurious interior a cocoon of warmth against the darkness outside. Kate gazed out the window at the scattered lights below, cities and towns reduced to glittering constellations against the black canvas of earth. From this height, the human world looked small, finite, beautiful, but fragile.

"Have you been to Paris before?" Devon asked, sensing her contemplative mood.

"No," Kate admitted. "I've always wanted to go. The Louvre, the artists in Montmartre…" She gave a hollow laugh. "Though I never imagined my first visit would be for a vampire tribunal."

Devon set aside the tablet he'd been reviewing and took her hand, his thumb tracing circles on her palm.

"I wish I could show it to you properly. Paris in the spring is magnificent, the gardens in bloom, the city alive with art and music."

"Maybe someday," Kate said, then paused, considering her words. "Although if I choose what I think I'm going to choose, we'd have all the time in the world to see Paris in every season, wouldn't we?"

Devon's hand stilled on hers. "Kate…"

"I've been thinking," she said, turning to face him fully. "About what you showed me last night. About what we really are to each other, and what I want our future to look like."

Devon's expression was carefully neutral, but she could see the hope and fear warring in his ancient eyes. "And what have you decided?"

Kate was quiet for a moment, gathering her thoughts. "I've spent my whole life feeling like I was waiting for something, like I was only living a half-life. With you, I feel like I'm finally becoming who I was always meant to be."

Devon's grip on her hand tightened. "Do you understand what you're saying? What you'd be giving up?"

"I'd be giving up a mortal life for an immortal one. I'd be giving up the limitations that have always held me back." Kate leaned closer to him. "Devon, I've seen what you are when you don't hold back. I've felt the power, the intensity, the sheer scope of what's possible. And I want that. Not because I want to be your equal, I understand now that equality isn't about matching power. It's about choosing each other completely."

Devon's eyes were bright with unshed tears. "Kate, once it's done, there's no going back. You would be changed forever."

"Good," Kate said firmly. "I don't want to go back. I want to go forward. With you."

Devon pulled her into his arms, holding her close. "Are you certain? Absolutely certain?"

Kate thought about her conversation with her mother. She thought about Zoe and the themes of transformation that had been emerging in her own work for months. She thought about the way she felt when Devon touched her, when he looked at her, when he trusted her with his darkest secrets.

"I'm certain," she said. "I want you to turn me, Devon. After we face the Council, after we deal with Elisabeta, I want you to make me like you."

Devon pulled back to look at her, his expression a mixture of joy and terror. "The Council will need to approve it. Turning someone without permission is now strictly forbidden."

Kate smiled, feeling a surge of confidence. "Then we'll ask them. We'll tell them that this is what I choose, what we both choose. And if they say no..." She shrugged. "Well, we'll cross that bridge when we come to it."

Devon laughed, a sound of pure amazement. "You continue to surprise me, Kate Morgan."

"Good," she said, pulling him down for a kiss. "I plan to keep you on your toes for the next few centuries."

The rest of the flight passed in comfortable conversation about their future, about the practicalities of immortality, about the life they would build together.

Paris at night was a breathtaking symphony of light and shadow. Kate pressed her face to the car window as it wound through historic streets, taking in the ornate architecture and history that flowed through every corner.

"It's beautiful," she whispered.

"Yes," Devon agreed, though his eyes were on her rather than the city outside. "Beautiful."

They were staying in an elegant apartment in the 6th arrondissement, arranged by Antoine's local contacts. The building dated from the 19th century, its high ceilings and parquet floors speaking of old-world luxury, while modern security systems provided the protection they needed.

"The Council chambers are beneath the city," Devon explained as they settled in. "Part of an ancient network of tunnels and catacombs that predates most of what you see above ground. The Carrières de Paris."

Kate shivered slightly at the thought. "A hidden world beneath the tourist attractions."

"Exactly. Vampires have always existed alongside humans, just… adjacent to their reality." Devon moved to the window, gazing out at the illuminated dome of the Panthéon in the distance. "The meeting is set for tomorrow night. We have until then to prepare."

Kate joined him at the window, wrapping her arms around his waist from behind. "We should explore the city tonight. If this might be my only visit to Paris, I want to see it properly."

Devon turned in her embrace, studying her face. "Are you sure? It might be safer to stay here."

"I'm tired of hiding," Kate said firmly. "Besides, we're supposed to be making our case that a vampire and human can coexist openly, aren't we? Let's practice what we preach."

A smile tugged at Devon's lips. "As always, your courage humbles me." He kissed her forehead. "Very well. Paris by night it is."

They spent the evening exploring the city of lights with Devon playing tour guide, pointing out landmarks and sharing his knowledge. Kate took it all in, from the grand opera house to the cafés where artists had met over the years. Below the surface of the tourist experience, however, Kate couldn't shake the feeling that someone was watching them. Occasionally, she would catch glimpses of figures in shadows, there one moment and gone the next. Devon noticed too, his posture becoming increasingly alert as the night wore on.

"Elisabeta's people?" Kate asked quietly as they paused on a bridge over the Seine.

Devon nodded, his eyes scanning the darkness. "And possibly Council observers as well. We're being evaluated even before the formal hearing."

They returned to the apartment earlier than planned, the weight of unseen eyes making their exploration less enjoyable than it should have been. As Devon secured the locks and activated the security system, a knock came at the door. They exchanged alarmed glances. No one should know they were here except Antoine's most trusted contacts. Devon motioned for Kate to stay back as he approached the door cautiously.

"Who is it?" he called.

"A friend," came the reply, a woman's voice with a faint accent Kate couldn't place. "I come with information you need to know for tomorrow night."

Devon hesitated, then checked the peephole. Whatever he saw made him relax significantly. He opened the door to reveal a slender woman with long blonde hair, her ageless face marking her as a vampire despite her modern attire.

"Sophia," Devon said, surprise evident in his voice. "I didn't expect to see you here."

"Clearly," she replied with a small smile. "May I come in? It's not wise to be seen visiting you."

Devon stepped aside, allowing her to enter. "Kate, you remember Sophia, from the Midwinter gathering? She's a member of the Council, the youngest, relatively speaking."

"Only six hundred years old," Sophia said with a self-deprecating shrug. "A mere child by Council standards. It's good to see you again, Kate."

Kate smiled, "You too, Sophia." Unlike Elisabeta's cunning grace or Antoine's controlled power, Sophia projected an air of scholarly intelligence, her eyes sharp and assessing behind stylish glasses she clearly didn't need.

"Why are you here?" Devon asked, his tone respectful but wary.

"To warn you," Sophia said simply. "The Council is divided on your case. Viktor is officially neutral, but three members are firmly against you, influenced by Elisabeta's testimony. Two, including myself, are sympathetic to your position."

"And the seventh?" Kate asked.

Sophia's gaze shifted to her, assessing. "Undecided. Which makes him the key to your fate."

Devon offered her a seat, and they gathered in the living room, the elegant furniture at odds with the gravity of their conversation.

"There's more," Sophia continued. "Aleksander has been gathering evidence against you. Photos documenting your relationship, moments that risk exposing our existence to humans."

Devon's expression darkened. "Aleksander? How?"

"He's been following you for months, it seems. Ever since Kate first came to your estate." Sophia's eyes were sympathetic. "The photos are… intimate. Private moments never meant to be shared."

Kate felt sick at the violation. She had known Aleksander was no friend of Devon's; their past as adversaries was well-established, but she thought they'd reached a mutual understanding and level of civility.

"He will pay for this," Devon said, his voice low and dangerous.

"Perhaps," Sophia agreed. "But first, you must survive the Council's judgment." She leaned forward, her expression earnest. "I'm telling you this so you won't be blindsided tomorrow. The evidence will be presented publicly. You need to be prepared."

"Thank you," Kate said, finding her voice. "But why help us? What do you gain?"

Sophia smiled and revealed the tips of her delicate fangs. "I believe our kind needs to evolve or we will perish. The world is changing. Technology makes it harder to stay hidden. We must change to survive." She turned to Devon. "Your relationship shows a possible future where vampires and humans live as equals, not as predator and prey."

"Not everyone shares your vision," Devon said.

"No," Sophia replied. "Many fear change. They fear losing the power that comes with equality." She stood up gracefully. "I have to go, it's risky for me to be seen here."

At the door, she paused, looking back at them. "There's something else you should know. I've heard rumors… communications between Aleksander and Elisabeta dating back months. I can't confirm it, but it seems his involvement may be deeper than simply gathering evidence."

Devon went still. "What are you suggesting?"

"That perhaps Aleksander's betrayal began long before this Council summons." Sophia's eyes were grave. "Be careful, Devon. Old acquaintances sometimes make the most dangerous enemies."

After Sophia left, Kate and Devon sat in silence, absorbing the implications of her warning.

"Aleksander and Elisabeta," Kate said finally, the connection sending a chill through her. "You don't think…"

"That he's the one who told her about you?" Devon's face was grim. "It would explain how she knew so much, so quickly. How she found us in New York."

"But why? What would he gain?"

Devon was quiet for a long moment, his jaw tight with something that looked like old, deep-seated pain. Kate squeezed his hands, sensing this was more than simple vampire politics.

"There's something I haven't told you about Aleksander," Devon said finally, his voice carefully controlled. "About our history. About her history with him."

Kate waited, recognizing the weight in his words, the confession he was about to make.

"Before she turned me," Devon began, his eyes fixed on a point in the distant past, "Aleksander was her Pet."

The words hung in the air, and Kate felt her breath catch.

"He was seventeen when he came into her service," Devon continued, his voice low and heavy with the weight of history. "For ten years, he was her devoted human companion. He served her, learned from her, believed that he was earning his place at her side. He thought she would make him her immortal partner."

"He loved her?" Kate questioned, the parallel to her own journey sending a cold dread through her.

"He wanted to be like her, a vampire." Devon corrected gently. "But she never saw him as an equal. Then she met me, a twenty-six-year-old musician . She saw something in me that she never saw in him. She turned me within months."

Kate's hands tightened on his. "And Aleksander?"

"She pushed him away," Devon said, the words bitter in his mouth. "He was twenty-seven. His whole youth had gone into serving a woman who treated him like just a passing distraction. He was turned down, shamed, and still human."

Kate could picture it with horrifying clarity: A young man, his devotion thrown back in his face, watching another receive the prize he had spent a decade striving for.

"He spent the next five years searching for another maker," Devon whispered. "He finally found one, Radu, a gutter king who ruled through fear. Aleksander struggled to survive in the bloodiest corners of our world. He had to fight his way up from nothing, all while believing I had received everything he was denied."

"But that's not true," Kate said fiercely, her loyalty flaring. "You've built your own life. You fought against her, you made your own choices. You are not her creation."

"I know that. You know that." Devon finally met her eyes, and the pain in them was raw and ancient. "But in Aleksander's mind? In his mind, I am the living symbol of his greatest humiliation. Every piece of respect I command, every territory I hold, every moment of happiness I find… he sees it as stolen from him. And you…"

He trailed off, his grip on her hands becoming almost painfully tight.

"Me?" Kate prompted softly.

"You are the ultimate insult," Devon said, his voice thick with emotion. "A Pet who he sees as having captured my heart. A partnership built on love and respect. You are everything he was denied, everything he was told he was unworthy of. He doesn't just want to hurt me, Kate. He wants to prove that his story is the only true story. That all Pets are objects to be discarded, and that our love is a lie."

Kate absorbed this, the full, horrifying picture finally clear. The venom in Aleksander's voice, his obsession and cruelty, was all the twisted reflection of a promise that was broken. She now understood why Sophia had seemed so concerned, why the warning about "old acquaintances" had carried such weight.

"He's not going to stop," she said. It wasn't a question.

"No," Devon said simply. "Aleksander doesn't know how to stop. He's been nursing this grievance for nearly four centuries. And now that he's found a way to strike at me through the Council, through Elisabeta, through you… he'll keep pushing until he's either proven his point or destroyed himself trying."

Kate took Devon's hands in hers, her resolve hardening. "We'll figure it out. But right now, we need to focus on the Council. On her."

His anger faded and was replaced by a grim determination. He nodded. "You're right. We should rest. Tomorrow will test us both."

But rest proved elusive for both of them; the pressure of tomorrow's judgment hung over them like a shadow as they got ready for bed. Kate moved slowly and purposefully, trying to savor every moment and sensation.

"Devon?" she said softly as they stood in the bedroom, the ornate space lit only by the soft glow of Parisian streetlights filtering through the curtains.

"Yes?" His voice was gentle, but she could hear the tension beneath it.

"Tomorrow, when we face the Council… there's a chance they might…" She couldn't finish the sentence, couldn't voice the possibility that they might be executed for their relationship.

Devon crossed to her, his hands coming up to frame her face. "There's a chance," he admitted quietly. "The Council has the power of life and death over our kind. And by extension, over those we love."

Kate felt tears prick her eyes. "Then this could be it. Tonight might be our last night together."

"It might be," Devon said, his thumb brushing away a tear that had escaped. "But Kate, even if it is, I want you to know that loving you has been the greatest privilege of my existence. You've given me more joy in these months than I've known in centuries."

Kate reached up to cover his hands with hers. "I love you," she whispered. "Whatever happens tomorrow, I need you to know that I chose this. I choose you. I choose us."

The kiss that followed was soft at first, tender and sweet, but it quickly deepened as the weight of their situation pressed down on them. This might be their last kiss, their last touch, their last moment to connect before the ancient laws of the vampire world put an end to them.

They undressed each other slowly, layer by layer, as if each revealed inch of skin was precious beyond measure. When Devon's shirt fell away, Kate skimmed the lines of his chest with her fingertips, memorizing the feel of him, the way his muscles tensed under her touch.

"You're so beautiful," she whispered, pressing her lips to his collarbone, tasting the salt of his skin.

Devon's breath hitched as her mouth moved lower, her tongue tracing patterns across his chest. His hands tangled in her hair, holding her close as if he could anchor himself to this moment, to her.

When her blouse joined his shirt on the floor, Devon's eyes darkened with desire and something deeper, a desperate need to claim her and mark this moment as theirs. His mouth found her throat, his fangs grazing her pulse point without breaking the skin.

"Kate," he murmured against her neck, her name spilling like silk from his lips. "My Kate."

She pressed into him, her body responding to his touch with an intensity that bordered on desperation. When his hands moved to the clasp of her bra, she helped him, needing to feel his skin against hers, needing the connection that only he could provide.

The rest of their clothes disappeared quickly with whispered endearments. Kate backed herself onto the bed slowly, and Devon settled down beside her. When they finally met on the bed, it felt intimate. It spoke of love, loss, passion, and the chance of goodbye. Devon's hands traced her body, appreciating every curve and every sensitive spot that made her gasp and arch under him. His mouth pressed kisses to her breasts, her ribs, the soft skin of her stomach.

"I want to remember everything," he said against her skin, his voice thick with emotion. "The way you taste, the way you feel, the sounds you make when I touch you here…" His fingers found the sensitive spot between her thighs, and Kate inhaled sharply, her hips bucking slightly off the bed.

"I need you, Devon," she gasped, her hands clutching at his shoulders. "I need all of you."

He moved up her body, his eyes locked on hers as he gently grabbed her jaw. "Look at me," he said softly. "I want to see your eyes when I fill you up."

Kate met his gaze as he entered her, slowly, carefully, as if she were made of the finest crystal. The sensation was overwhelming, not just the physical pleasure, but the emotional weight of the moment, the knowledge that this might be their last time together.

They moved together with a desperate tenderness, each thrust a declaration of love. Devon's hands never stopped roaming her body; he stroked her hair, caressed her face, and held her as if she might disappear at any moment. Fueled by desperate need, their rhythm increased. When Kate's orgasm took hold, it was with Devon's name on her lips and tears streaming down her cheeks. Devon followed moments later, burying his face in her neck as his body shuddered with the force of his climax.

They lay entwined together, Devon still inside Kate, neither willing to break the connection. Devon's fingers traced lazy patterns on Kate's bare shoulder, while she listened to the sound of light rain hitting the windows.

"Whatever happens tomorrow," Kate said softly, "I want you to know that this, us, it's been worth everything. Every risk, every danger, every moment of fear. You've been worth it all."

Devon's arms tightened around her. "Kate…"

"No," she said, pressing a finger to his lips. "Let me say this. If the Council decides against us, if this is our last night together, I want you to know that I've never been happier than I've been with you. You've shown me what it means to truly live and love without reservation. If I die tomorrow, I'll die knowing that I was loved completely by the most extraordinary creature I've ever known."

Devon caught her hand, pressing it to his lips. "You're not going to die," he said fiercely. "I won't let them take you from me."

"You might not have a choice," Kate said gently. "But Devon, if something happens to me, I need you to promise me something."

"Anything."

"Promise me you won't let this destroy you. Promise me you'll find a way to be happy again, even if it takes centuries."

Devon was quiet for a long moment, his jaw clenched with emotion. "I can't promise that," he said finally. "Because a world without you in it isn't a world I want to exist in."

Kate felt fresh tears spring to her eyes. "Devon..."

"I've lived for centuries, Kate," he continued, his voice raw and honest. "Centuries of emptiness, of going through the motions of existing without truly living. You brought color back to my world. You gave me a reason to want to see another decade, another century. Without you..." He shook his head. "There would be no point. I would choose to join you, wherever you went."

They made love again as dawn approached, slower this time, savoring each touch, each kiss, each whispered word of love. When exhaustion finally claimed them, they fell asleep wrapped in each other's arms, holding tight to their last moments of peace before facing the judgment of the vampire Council.

While the sun rose over Paris, painting the sky in shades of gold and rose, Kate and Devon slept the sleep of the condemned, their bodies intertwined, their love a bright flame against the darkness that threatened to snuff them out.

The evening would bring the Council, the judgment, and possibly the end of everything they had built together. But last night had been theirs, and their alone.

Chapter 21

The entrance to the Council chambers was hidden beneath an unassuming building on the Île de la Cité. A bookshop on the ground floor provided cover for the elevator that descended deep below the city streets, accessed through a back room protected by modern security.

Kate felt the weight of earth above them as they descended, the air growing cooler and somehow older with each passing second. Devon stood next to her in a fitted black suit. His face was calm, but his eyes betrayed his feelings. "Whatever happens, we face it together," he whispered softly into her ear. Kate nodded and smoothed the front of her blue knee-length dress. It projected confidence, even though she felt quite the opposite inside. Around her neck, Devon's mother's pendant rested against her skin, a small comfort in the face of the unknown.

The elevator doors opened to reveal a vaulted antechamber carved from the bedrock beneath the city. Torches in iron sconces provided flickering illumination, their light reflecting off the polished stone floor. A vampire attendant in formal attire waited to escort them.

"The Council is assembled," he informed them with a slight bow. "You will be called when they are ready."

They were led to a small waiting room, furnished with antique chairs and a table bearing a crystal decanter, which Kate suspected contained blood. Devon remained standing, too tense to sit, his eyes fixed on the heavy wooden doors that separated them from the Council chamber.

"Devon," Kate said softly, taking his hand. "It's going to be alright."

He looked down at her, his ancient eyes filled with a vulnerability that made her heart ache. "I've faced many dangers in my long life, Kate. But never have I had so much to lose."

Before she could respond, the doors swung open. The attendant reappeared, his expression solemn.

"The Council will see you now."

The chamber inside resembled Roman architecture with its domed ceiling and columned perimeter. Seven regal chairs were arranged in a semicircle on a raised platform, each occupied by a figure who radiated power and age in a way that made Kate's human instincts scream danger.

In the center chair sat Viktor Dracul, whom she recognized from the Midwinter Gathering in Budapest. Unlike the others, whose appearances ranged from middle-aged to elderly, Viktor looked no more than forty, tall and lean with sharp features and eyes so dark they appeared black. His presence dominated the room, a gravity that seemed to bend space around him.

To Viktor's right sat Elisabeta, dressed in crimson, her smile like a blade as she watched Devon and Kate approach. And beside her, to Kate's shock and fury, was Aleksander, standing obediently behind Elisabeta's chair like a favored servant.

"Devon Karlov," Viktor's voice filled the chamber, deep and ringing with the weight of centuries. "You stand before this Council accused of endangering vampire secrecy through your relationship with a human. How do you respond?"

Devon stepped forward, his posture straight and proud. "I deny the accusation, Lord Dracul. My relationship with Katherine Morgan poses no threat to our society or its secrets."

A murmur ran through the assembled vampires who lined the walls of the chamber, observers to the proceedings, Kate realized. Some nodded in agreement with Devon's statement; others scoffed openly.

"Bold words," said an elderly-looking vampire to Viktor's left. "But we have evidence that suggests otherwise."

At a gesture from Viktor, Aleksander stepped forward, producing a leather portfolio. "With the Council's permission," he said, his voice smooth and practiced, "I present documentation of Devon Karlov's reckless behavior with the human Katherine Morgan."

Kate watched in horror as Aleksander showed a series of photographs on a large screen at the side of the chamber. Images of her and Devon together in intimate moments that were never meant for public viewing. Their private world was exposed for these ancient figures to judge and condemn. Devon's hand found hers and squeezed tightly as they faced the violation together. His face remained impassive, but she could feel the rage radiating from him in waves.

"As you can see," Aleksander continued, "they make no attempt to conceal their relationship. They appear in public together. The human knows everything about our kind, our strengths, our weaknesses, and our society. She is a walking security breach."

"Is this true?" Viktor asked, his dark eyes fixed on Devon. "Does she know everything?"

"She knows what she needs to know," Devon replied carefully. "Katherine has proven herself trustworthy. She has kept our secrets even at risk to herself."

"Humans cannot be trusted," declared another Council member, a severe-looking woman with silver hair. "History has proven this time and again. They fear what they do not understand, and they destroy what they fear."

"With respect, Elder," Devon countered, "history also shows that humans can transcend their own limitations. Katherine has demonstrated loyalty, courage, and discretion that would honor any vampire."

Elisabeta laughed, the sound like crystal bells in the stone chamber. "How charming. He truly believes his Pet is special."

Devon's jaw tightened, but he maintained his composure. "Katherine is not my Pet. She is my partner, my lover. My equal."

This caused a greater stir among the observers. Even some Council members shifted uncomfortably at the declaration.

"Equal?" Elisabeta's voice dripped with mockery. "A fragile human, equal to a vampire? She will be dust while you remain unchanged. What equality can exist in such a relationship?"

"The equality of choice," Devon said firmly. "Of mutual respect. Of love freely given and received."

Viktor leaned forward, his interest visibly piqued. "You speak of love, Devon Karlov. A rare admission from one of our kind."

"I speak the truth, Lord Dracul. As you commanded."

Viktor's gaze shifted to Kate, assessing her with eyes that had quite possibly witnessed millennia. "And you, Katherine Morgan. What do you say to these accusations? Are you a threat to our kind?"

Kate straightened her spine, feeling the weight of ancient gazes upon her. "I am not a threat, Elder Dracul," she said, her voice steadier than she had expected. "I have kept your secrets and will continue to do so. Not out of fear, but out of respect for Devon and for the society he belongs to."

"Bold words from a human in a room full of vampires," observed a younger-looking Council member, Sophia, Kate realized. "She stands before us without trembling. She speaks with conviction. These are not the actions of one who would betray secrets out of fear or weakness."

"Or perhaps it merely demonstrates her foolishness," countered the silver-haired woman. "Humans are notoriously poor judges of danger."

"May I speak further, Elder Dracul?" Kate asked, addressing Viktor directly.

Viktor studied her for a long moment, then nodded. "You may."

Kate took a deep breath, gathering her thoughts. "I understand your concerns. From your perspective, I'm a security risk. But I would argue that my relationship with Devon represents an opportunity, not a threat."

"Go on," Viktor prompted.

"Technology is making it harder for any group to remain completely hidden." Kate said, echoing Sophia's words from the previous night. "The future lies not in hidden secrecy, but in controlled integration. Finding humans who can be trusted and who can bridge the gap between our worlds."

A murmur ran through the chamber at her words. Kate continued with growing confidence. "I'm an artist. I understand the power of narrative. Right now, human stories about vampires are based on fear and fantasy. What if there could be new stories of cooperation and mutual benefit?"

"Dangerous ideas," growled one of the Council members.

"Visionary ones," countered Sophia.

Viktor raised a hand, silencing the debate. "You speak well for a human, Katherine Morgan. But words are easy. Actions prove intent." He turned to Devon. "Your maker has raised serious concerns about your judgment in this matter."

Elisabeta smiled, triumph gleaming in her amber eyes. "I have only the best interests of our society at heart, Lord Dracul. My creation has always been impulsive. Prone to emotional decisions that endanger himself and others."

"That is not true," Devon said, his voice tight with controlled anger. "Elisabeta's concern is not for vampire society, but for her own control. She cannot accept that I have found happiness beyond her influence."

"You dare question my motives?" Elisabeta hissed, her composure cracking slightly.

"I state facts," Devon replied coldly. "You have manipulated, threatened, and interfered in my life for centuries. This complaint to the Council is merely your latest attempt to reassert control over me."

Viktor watched this exchange with interest, his ancient eyes moving between Devon and Elisabeta. "The connection between maker and progeny is complex," he observed. "But it does not grant absolute authority in perpetuity. Devon Karlov has lived independently for centuries, establishing himself as a respected member of our society."

Elisabeta's smile faltered slightly at this implicit rebuke.

"However," Viktor continued, turning back to Devon and Kate, "your relationship with this human is why we are gathered tonight. The evidence presented shows a concerning disregard for discretion."

He rose from his chair, his movement fluid despite his immense age. The other Council members followed suit, a clear signal that the public portion of the proceedings was complete.

"We will deliberate," Viktor announced. "Devon Karlov, Katherine Morgan, you will wait for our decision."

As the Council members filed out through a side door, Elisabeta paused beside Kate, leaning close to whisper in her ear.

"Enjoy these last moments with him," she murmured, her cool breath raising goosebumps on Kate's skin. "One way or another, he will return to me. He always does."

Before Kate could respond, Elisabeta glided away, following the other Council members. Aleksander trailed after her, carefully avoiding Devon's murderous gaze. Left alone in the chamber except for a few attendants, Devon and Kate moved to a stone bench along the wall. The observers had been dismissed, leaving the space eerily quiet.

"You were magnificent," Devon said softly, taking her hand. "I've never heard anyone address the Council with such courage."

"I was terrified," Kate said, her voice shaking.

Devon rubbed circles on her palm, a gesture that always made her feel better. "No matter what they decide, Kate, know I am proud to stand beside you. I am proud to call you mine."

Kate leaned against him, drawing comfort from his presence. "Do you think we convinced them?"

"Some, perhaps. Sophia was already sympathetic." I think Viktor was intrigued by your perspective." Devon sighed. "But the traditionalists will be harder to sway."

They sat in silence after that, the minutes stretching into an hour, then two. The waiting was its own form of torture, each passing moment ratcheting up the tension until Kate felt she might shatter from it. Finally, a door opened, and Antoine slipped into the chamber, his expression urgent.

"Devon," he said in a low voice, approaching them quickly. "I need to speak with you. Now."

Devon exchanged a glance with Kate, then stood. "What is it?"

"Not here," Antoine insisted, gesturing toward a small antechamber.

Devon hesitated, clearly reluctant to leave Kate alone, but she nodded encouragingly.

"Go. I'll be fine."

Once inside the antechamber, Antoine pulled out a smartphone. Technology seemed oddly out of place in these ancient surroundings.

"Look at this," Antoine said, showing Devon the screen. "My contacts intercepted these communications between Aleksander and Elisabeta. They go back months, well before she reappeared in New York."

Devon's face went still as he read, his expression hardening into something cold and dangerous. "He's been planning this for the better part of a year," he said finally, his voice barely controlled. "He told her about Kate from the beginning."

"Not just told her," Antoine corrected. "He's been manipulating both of you. He fed Elisabeta information while pretending to be your ally. He set up this entire Council hearing."

"Why?" Devon demanded. "What does he gain?"

"Your territory, your status, your place in vampire society," Antoine said grimly. "He's been setting himself up to regain Elisabeta's favor. If you're disgraced or executed, he stands to inherit everything you've built."

Devon's hands turned into fists, and his control was clearly slipping. "I'll kill him."

"Not here," Antoine warned. "Not now. The Council is returning. But Devon, be careful. Aleksander has clearly been playing a long game. He may have other moves we haven't anticipated."

They returned to the main chamber just as the side door opened and the Council members filed back in. Kate stood as Devon rejoined her, immediately sensing the change in him, barely contained fury radiating from his tense form.

"What is it?" she whispered.

"Later," Devon murmured, his eyes fixed on Aleksander, who had resumed his position behind Elisabeta's chair.

The Council members took their seats, their ancient faces impassive. Viktor remained standing, his dark gaze sweeping over the chamber before settling on Devon and Kate.

"Devon Karlov, Katherine Morgan, approach," he commanded.

They stood together, hands still joined, and moved to stand before the Council. Kate could feel the weight of seven archaic gazes upon her, judging, assessing, deciding her fate.

Viktor's voice echoed through the chamber, "We have considered your case carefully. The relationship between vampires and humans has always been complicated. Our laws exist to protect our society from exposure and the chaos that would follow if our existence became widely known."

He paused, his dark eyes shifting between them. "However, we also recognize that times change." That adaptation is sometimes necessary for survival."

A flicker of hope kindled in Kate's chest at these words.

"The Council is divided on your case," Viktor continued. "Some see your relationship as a dangerous precedent that threatens our secrecy. Others see potential in a new approach to human-vampire relations."

Elisabeta frowned as Viktor spoke. Sophia seemed cautiously optimistic. Devon turned his attention to Aleksander, who stood just behind Elisabeta's chair. Their eyes met across the room, and for a brief moment, Aleksander's mask slipped. A quick look of triumph crossed his face, confirming everything. This was his plan all along. He aimed to use Elisabeta's obsession with Devon as a weapon to manipulate the Council into destroying what Devon had built, so he could take advantage of the resulting void. Devon tightened his grip on Kate's hand. His rage simmered just beneath his calm exterior. She squeezed back, reminding him of what was at stake.

"The deciding vote falls to me as head of this Council." Viktor's voice brought Devon's focus back to the meeting. "But before I cast it, I have one final question." He stared at Devon, intense and steady. "Devon Karlov, what are your ultimate intentions toward Katherine Morgan?"

The question had clear implications for everyone present. Devon's answer would determine their fates. Kate felt Devon's hand tighten around hers as he faced Viktor's stare. The chamber was silent, every vampire present waiting for his response. Devon looked at Kate, their eyes meeting in complete understanding and devotion. Then he turned back to Viktor, his decision made.

"My intentions, Lord Dracul," Devon began, his voice steady and clear, "are to love her, to honor her, and to protect her. I will cherish her human life for as long as she chooses to live it. But should she, of her own free will, choose to join me in eternity, I will be the one to turn her. Her future, like her heart, is entwined with mine."

The declaration was bold, a direct claim of love and intent that left the Council momentarily stunned. Viktor's gaze, cold and piercing, shifted from Devon to Kate.

"A touching sentiment. But let's be clear and frank." He leaned forward, his voice a dangerous whisper. "Do you, human, truly wish to become one of us? Do you want to become vampire?"

Kate's heart hammered against her ribs. She felt Devon's hand tighten, a silent offer of support. She met Viktor Dracul's gaze and took a deep breath, her voice clear and steady.

"Yes," she said, her gaze unwavering. "I want to be turned."

A ripple of murmurs went through the chamber. Then, Kate turned her head, her eyes locking with Devon's, a silent promise passing between them.

"Turned by Devon."

Viktor's obsidian eyes narrowed, a flicker of something resembling admiration in their depths. He turned his gaze to Elisabeta, whose triumphant smirk had curdled into an expression of stunned disbelief.

"What troubles me more is not Devon's choice of companion, but your continued interference in his existence."

Elisabeta's composure faltered. "My lord?"

"Four centuries, Elisabeta." Viktor's voice dropped lower, becoming more dangerous. "For four centuries, you have used the maker bond to toy with him. To punish him for seeking independence. To assert control long after any reasonable maker would have released their progeny."

The chamber grew colder as Viktor stepped closer to Elisabeta. "Did you think we were unaware? That the Council does not see how you abuse the sacred trust of the maker bond?"

Elisabeta's face betrayed a flicker of fear. "My lord, I have only exercised my rights as—"

"Rights?" Viktor's laugh was cold and sharp as broken glass. "The maker bond is not a right. It is a responsibility. A sacred trust to guide, to teach, and then to release."

He gestured toward Devon. "This progeny has existed for centuries. He has built wealth, power, and reputation. He has never endangered our kind or broken our laws. Yet you maintain your hold, pulling his strings like a puppet master when it amuses you."

Kate watched as Viktor circled Elisabeta. The ancient vampire seemed to grow larger, his shadow stretching across the chamber floor.

"The Council has deliberated," Viktor continued, "and we find your behavior unbecoming of one of your age and standing. You dishonor the traditions you claim to protect."

Fear flickered across Elisabeta's face, her composure cracking. "My lord, I—"

Viktor's voice took on a formal, ritual quality that made the air in the chamber vibrate, "By the authority vested in me as First of the Council, I command you to release Devon Karlov from your maker bond. Now. In this chamber. Before these witnesses."

A collective gasp rose from the shadowy Council members. Kate felt Devon stiffen beside her, his hand gripping hers so tightly it almost hurt.

"Release him?" Elisabeta's voice rose, her carefully maintained poise shattering. "My lord, you cannot—"

"I can and I do." Viktor's eyes flashed crimson. "You have abused the most sacred connection between our kind. You have used it not to guide but to torment. Not to teach but to control."

He gestured dismissively. "You treat a centuries-old vampire like a child's toy, picking him up and discarding him at your whim. This is beneath you, Elisabeta. It diminishes you in the eyes of the Council."

Elisabeta's face contorted with rage and disbelief. "He is mine! By blood and by law!"

"He was yours to guide, not to own," Viktor corrected coldly. "The time for guidance ended centuries ago."

He turned to address the shadowy figures behind him. "The Council recognizes that the severing of a maker bond is not undertaken lightly. But when the bond has been corrupted, when it serves only the maker's vanity and cruelty, it must be broken."

Viktor returned his attention to Elisabeta, his voice dropping to a danger-ous whisper. "You will release him. Now. Or you will be brought before this Council to answer for your defiance. And I assure you, Elisabeta, you do not wish to stand before me in judgment."

The threat hung in the air, palpable and cold. For a long moment, Elisabeta remained silent, her eyes burning with hatred as she stared at Devon. Finally, Elisabeta spoke, each word seeming to cause her physical pain.

"I, Elisabeta Ardelean, release you, Devon Karlov, from our maker bond."

The effect was immediate and visible. Devon gasped, his body jerking as if struck by an invisible force. His hand flew to his throat, to the mark that had bound him to Elisabeta for four centuries. Before Kate's eyes, the silvery pattern began to fade, the edges blurring and dissolving like frost under morning sun.

"It is done," Viktor said with finality. "The bond is broken."

Elisabeta trembled with barely contained fury, but she bowed her head. "As the Council commands," she said, each word dripping with venom.

"Furthermore," Viktor continued, "you will cease all actions against Devon Karlov and his human companion immediately. You will recall any agents you have set in motion. You will withdraw completely from their affairs."

He leaned closer to her, his voice carrying to every corner of the chamber. "And know this, Elisabeta. The Council's eyes are upon you now. Every shadow you cast, every whisper you utter, every move you make—we will be watching."

Elisabeta's eyes widened before she composed herself, bowed, and left the chamber with what little dignity and pride she had left. The chamber fell silent. Kate could hear her own heartbeat pounding in her ears. Next to her, Devon remained frozen, his hand still at his throat, looking stunned. Viktor turned to them, his ancient eyes focusing on Devon.

"Four centuries is long enough to be bound to one such as her," he said, his voice gentler now. "You should have come to the Council sooner."

"I did not believe..." Devon began, then stopped, collecting himself. "I did not believe the Council would intervene in a maker-progeny dispute."

Kate felt Devon's hand tighten around hers again, but this time not from tension, from wonder. She could see it in his eyes, the realization that for the first time in four centuries, his mind was truly his own. Viktor nodded once, then turned back to the shadowy Council.

"This matter is concluded. The Council's judgment has been rendered."

As he passed Kate, he paused, his dark gaze met hers. "Miss Morgan, when next we meet at our gatherings, I trust it will be as one reborn into our world. Choose your moment wisely."

The words were both a blessing and a warning, an acknowledgment of her decision and a reminder of its gravity. Devon and Kate walked away from the Council chambers, hand in hand, into the cool Paris night. The weight of the world seemed to lift, replaced by a giddy sense of relief. They had won. They had faced down his maker, the entire Council, and had come out the other side unharmed.

"I can't believe it," Kate breathed, leaning against him as they stood on a quiet, ancient street. "We're safe."

"For now," Devon murmured, pulling her into a fierce, triumphant kiss. It was a kiss of victory, of relief, of a future suddenly, gloriously, returned to them. "Let's go home."

He hailed their car, a classic black sedan appeared out of the shadows. He opened the door for Kate, his smile never leaving his face. She slid into the back seat, her own heart soaring with a joy she hadn't realized she'd been missing. She looked up, expecting Devon to follow her in.

Instead, the door slammed shut. The locks clicked.

Before Kate could even process what was happening, two figures emerged from the front seats, vampires she didn't recognize, their faces grim and stoic. The car sped away from the curb, pinning her to the seat. She twisted around, her eyes wide with terror, and looked out the rear window. She saw Devon, his triumphant expression turning to one of dawning horror as he realized the drivers weren't his. He started to run, but the car was already accelerating, weaving into the Parisian traffic with supernatural skill.

Then she saw him.

Aleksander.

Stepping out of the shadows where the car had been waiting, he met her gaze through the glass. He wore a cruel and triumphant smile across his face. He raised a hand in a mocking wave. The car turned a corner, and Devon was gone. Kate was alone, trapped and speeding into the darkness with her new, true enemy.

Thank You For Reading

If you enjoyed reading *The Partner* as much as I enjoyed writing it, please consider leaving a review!

https://www.amazon.com/dp/B0FL24TZX2

Acknowledgments

To my husband, for his never-ending support, for being the rock that tethers me to the earth, you mean everything to me.

To Claire from @tropeytrinkets, thank you for believing in this little indie author and being an incredible cheerleader for the Captive Hearts series.

To Gill and the gang at my local gym for listening to me go on and on about the books during group class.

To you, the reader, thank you for letting Devon and Kate into your world. I hope you've fallen in love with them as much as I have. Thank you for your support.

About The Author

Samantha Beneke is a South African-born writer who now calls New Zealand home. With a background in Media & Communications, she has spent her career crafting compelling narratives across multiple platforms, from digital marketing campaigns to literary publications.

Samantha's writing journey began early, earning recognition as a published teenage poet through several publications with the prestigious Douglas Livingstone Poetry competition in South Africa. Her talent for weaving words into powerful emotional experiences has continued throughout her career, with numerous magazine articles and online publications showcasing her versatility as a writer.

When she's not writing, Samantha continues to work in digital marketing, always seeking new ways to connect with audiences and tell stories that matter.

To follow her work and receive updates visit samanthabenekeromanceau thor.com

https://www.facebook.com/supernaturalromanceauthor/
https://www.tiktok.com/@samantha_beneke
https://www.instagram.com/supernaturalromanceauthor/

Other Books By Samantha Beneke

THE CAPTIVE HEARTS SERIES

- Pet - Book One

https://www.amazon.com/stores/Samantha-Beneke/author/B0FHJ7ZXJD